INNOCENTS ABROAD

A Novel of Florence

JUAN E. CORRADI

Fulton Books, Inc.
Meadville, PA

Published by Fulton Books 2021

ISBN 978-1-63710-588-7 (paperback)
ISBN 978-1-63710-589-4 (digital)

Printed in the United States of America

In memory of Magdalen Nabb

PREFACE

In times of plague, many of us withdraw to places we deem safe and, if we have the means, try to survive with a company we trust, and partake the joys of storytelling. During the Black Death in Tuscany, Boccaccio secluded himself with agreeable companions in the country—probably in one of the estates designated as a refuge by the hospital order of Santa Maria della Scala, in Siena. The product—the *Decameron*—became famous and has survived into our own days.

In these latter days, however, the entire world penetrates into the innermost recesses of any hideout, and turns us often into captive spectators of what's happening *urbi et orbi*. Passive consumption of tales takes precedence over storytelling. But the art is not lost, and it is great solace to practice and to share it. It is in this spirit that I have written what follows, as I am eager to tell a story. In a concession to the times, I have framed it as if it were a TV miniseries for the ubiquitous Netflix. Here it goes.

The story you are about to read is an invention, based like all inventions, on facts. The title is a nod to Mark Twain. The text mimics the labyrinthine shape of *La invención de Morel*, by Adolfo Bioy Casares (Borges's loyal friend) or at least the latter's three-part structure. The characters and situations are always fictitious, even when they hide behind real names. I am fully aware of the risks in a *roman à clef*. I do not wish to succumb to the shabby satisfaction of winking at a few who know who is who and what is what, because a few years hence, nobody will care. As in a portrait painting, the characters who pose are just a pretext to present shapes and colors and situations that have a life of their own and point to more universal themes.

The story seemingly has no plot, but it does have one: it is the saga of broken expectations by an accidental tourist of his times, who meets in his meandering other victims of disappointment but still finds the whole thing funny. Like Voltaire's *Candide*, in the end, he, or what remains of him, is contented to tend his own garden and leave the rest to self-destruct.

Yes, it is satire. It is presented as a series of episodes befitting a passage, and they follow a personal sequence: arrival, entrapment, release. Behind the sequence lies the plot. It is what happens when several trajectories intersect: the life of a long-lived villa (a composite of many, with a life so long that the object becomes a subject) and the shorter phase in the life of some of its inhabitants—both living and dead. The intersecting trajectories have one thing in common: the meltdown of high aspirations, piled one upon another, or reversion to the mean. As a sociologist, I can provide the statistical expression of the process. As a simple writer, I will say it is the saga of *a perennial return to mediocrity* (with a nod to Flaubert).

The thread is old Ariadne's string. The central character, however, is not only a person; it is also a house, majestic and sad, and excessively old. The person is only a foreman of a literary demolition squad pulling down a condemned building—chilly, deceptive, and, behind an imposing facade, unhealthy, cruel, and in the end, fatuous.

I harbor the hope that one day this text will be used as a script for the stage, or as a series of episodes for TV. Like in all librettos, each scene is but the tip of an iceberg. Underneath lies a mass of intrigues of glory and of gore.

ACKNOWLEDGMENTS

My special thanks to the following friends for their very helpful comments, edits, and suggestions: Paolo Bruni, Margherita Ciacci, Volker Meja, Bro Uttal, and Alexander Zaslavsky.

CAST OF CHARACTERS

1. The narrator
2. The villa
3. The first baron
4. The second baron
5. The third baron (ghost)
6. The first baron's wife (ghost)
7. The second baron's secretary
8. Art dealers
9. Tosca
10. Jack
11. A variegated chorus of innocents and crooks

SEASON 1
The Outsider

EPISODE 1

In Which Candido Bigordi Describes How He Became an Expatriate and a Citizen of the World

"Today I'm gonna enter my past—the past of my life." But through which door, and when? The tango *Los Mareados* uses a different pronoun: "*Hoy* vas *a entrar en mi pasado, en el pasado de mi vida.*" Today *you*'re gonna enter my past. It is addressed to a former lover. It declares somewhat sharply a separation, perhaps an execution. But if I say "*Hoy voy a entrar en mi pasado, en el pasado de mi vida,*" "today *I'm* gonna enter in my past," the phrase signals a return to oneself, perhaps a reunion." That is what Candido, in old age, when all loves had faded away, thought of himself.

It could be in the South of Buenos Aires, in the barrio of Barracas: the long entrance corridor on the *avenida* Montes de Oca, the garden in the back, the pigeons circling in formation over the trees, the balcony on the first floor, the large bedroom that opened on it, and from which he could hear the tramways running each way, accelerating and decelerating as the driver moved a lever on a metal disc to mark the speed points. It was on this balcony that he saw and heard the loads of *cabecitas negras* (so called because their faces were darker than the faces of those who ruled the country) chanting songs in support of Juan Perón as they moved toward Plaza de Mayo. "*Sin galera y sin bastón, los muchachos de Perón*" ("Without top hats and canes, we are Peron's boys")—the first rhyme he ever learned.

That was October 17, 1945. He was born two years earlier, when the golden years of Argentina—*con galera y con bastón,* as top hats and canes were de rigueur at the official ceremonies of the oligarchs—came to an end. That very day, the optimistic, eclectic, obscenely rich, pretentious, and much-celebrated Argentine *belle époque* suddenly stopped. A fitful authoritarian and populist era began.

Many decades passed, and Candido was afraid that he would die under that second era's dilapidated spell as well. Or perhaps, like Peruvian poet Cesar Vallejo, he would die regardless and elsewhere on a rainy day, on some day he could already remember.

> *Me moriré en París con aguacero,*
> *un día del cual tengo ya el recuerdo.*
> *Me moriré en París—y no me corro—*
> *tal vez un jueves, como es hoy, de otoño.*
>
> I will die in Paris, on a rainy day,
> on some day I can already remember.
> I will die in Paris—and I don't step aside—
> perhaps on a Thursday, as today is Thursday, in autumn.

Little Matteo, Candido's grandnephew, had entered the inquisitive age. Tio Candido was telling him some stories of a world that was and of a world to come. He told him how he remembered the first, and also the second.

"But Tio how can you remember something that has not yet happened?"

"Matteo, because what will happen has happened already."

"And what has happened will happen again?"

"Look, take this long strip of paper, twist it, and join the two ends. Then run your finger along it."

"It has only one side!"

"The same is true with time: past, present, and future are on the same plane."

"And the dead?"

14

"The dead and the living are on the same plane too. The dead always come back, and us, the living, are on vacation from death."

"Don't the dead go to a different place, one we cannot see, heaven or hell?"

"It's all the same; all there is this, the world around us. There is no heaven or hell, just a purgatory without end. In it we always think we could do better, and do worse."

If Candido entered his past through this door, the one of child-hood, it would seem like the one and only beginning. There is never such a thing—a single chain of events. It is a biographical illusion. In his particular case, the chain kept breaking, and he kept start-ing anew. Such a biography would consist of nothing but many first chapters. That happens to someone who has been always a stranger.

No. He'd rather compress his life into a compact single sentence composed of surprising turns and then pick one of those turns—the Florentine turn. Only in baroque fiction, a version of eternal return, could he find some truth. And so he imagined what a surviving friend might say, on a day of his death that he could already remember in his imagination. He wrote it down:

"Call me Chelito, as I was first called by the family, or just Candido. My friend could be Mito, Julio, or Roberto. I prefer Mito, and he says in his eulogy:

"That a boy from Barracas, a southern neighborhood of the city of Santa Maria del Buen Ayre, recalled in a milonga:

> *Barracas al Sur,*
> *Barracas al Norte,*
> *A mi me gusta*
> *Bailar con corte.*

> Southern Barracas,
> Northern Barracas,
> I love to dance
> With a broken step.

"A short, shy, and at school sometimes a shunned waif, an incomplete pianist with no other solace in his childhood than an infatuation with pirates and great discoverers, a voracity for languages, a belief in reincarnation, a deft hand drafting with pencil, and a passion for model airplanes, should become a professor in universities of the first world and, later in life, an offshore captain, an interpreter for various presidents, the confidant of a king and nearly a king himself, the lover of daughters of barons and generals, and nieces of cardinals, the disciple of German philosophers, the friend of several litterateurs who lived in Paris and of assorted billionaires who played in St. Moritz, a guest of embassies in the most exotic realms, a collector of boats and pearls, an avid handler of jeweled braveries, gold brocades, brooches and garlands with gold and topaz, and of carbuncles which glitter on the breasts, and of some of those breasts as well, the curator in chief of a Renaissance estate, a political leader manqué, a connoisseur of slow food paired with good wines, and the subject of several cloak-and-dagger escapades, would seem at first look far-fetched."

The sentence left Candido out of breath, so he stopped for a moment, and then let Mito continue.

"To those who understandably think so, I can attest that I knew Candido well, and I should like to recount part of his story, the part during which he lived in an old Florentine palace, became intrigued and familiar with people who were dead, and was harassed by others who were alive. The experience was intense, and triggered in him haunting memories, dark forebodings, and grand hopes.

"When Candido was a schoolboy in Argentina, at the very Scottish Southern District British School (formerly St. Andrews), he sometimes wanted to escape his native land, to visit places and times that were far away.

"He never was really at home. His country and his city were prosperous before they became preposterous, at the time quite humdrum we could say, except for the colorful rulers, who harangued the people from a balcony (he was a smiling military macho; she a resplendent vaudeville queen). The rude public of those days was being marched over a cliff by a couple of well-off adventurers posing as man and woman of the people. The tradition continued for decades after them, and the country never recovered, wasting its vast resources time and again—a nation underdeveloped through its own persistent efforts.

"In Candido's nightmares, the land and the people were ablaze with fire and brimstone. Many years later, a survivor of cataclysmic events, he thought his childhood dreams were premonitions, and that a sensible man should run away from such a place, though he cannot ultimately escape the clutches of its fate. Now the whole world is ablaze, so his premonitions were like the off-Broadway rehearsal of a drama that would play one day on the big stage. In the East and in the West, a diverse bunch of rich elitist carpetbaggers—military and civilian, businessmen and thieves, religious or secular, right and left—have learnt the art of posing as leaders of the people. And the morons follow them. In the UK, millions of Britons voted for the blitz, and in America, millions of turkeys voted for Thanksgiving.

"Childhood passed, and his path diverged from that of childhood friends. He left the country when he was still a teenager, and returned only on rare occasions, with ever-longer lapses in between. He kept his childhood city oceans apart but revisited it from time to time. Abroad or at home, everywhere he was perceived as being in a group but not of the group. He was intimate and withdrawn, close yet far from the people with whom he lived.

"He sometimes met some of the old acquaintances under more benevolent skies. There are few pleasures as great as good friendships resumed. 'As we said yesterday,' they joked. But that was as far as it went. Because of this gift or curse, his incurable estrangement, he could carry out tasks that no one else could do or hold conversations that could not be held between two full members of the group.

"In Florence, Candido was commissioned to carry one of those tasks: to restore a grand estate and turn it into an institute to explore advanced geopolitics and policies, and advanced culture as well, a bridge between Europe and America, and between them and the world. His bosses paid lip service to the view, but they were concerned mostly with the bottom line: how to bring many undergraduates to Florence, and hence free dormitory beds in the home campus. So in his naively noble quest, Candido was thwarted at every step.

"In that provincial and universal city Candido, who everyone thought was the lucky resident of a grandiose house, was in fact the inmate of a golden cage, a palace full of secrets, so rich and dismal and deep that he came to believe first that, trapped in a labyrinth, he would never be capable of leaving it, and that in all of the princely abode's exaggerated history, he was always there and had been nowhere else. It took a bit of courage, and a tour de force, to escape. The outsider went outside again. His enemies were actually his allies in the success of the feat.

"Candido's basic mistake was his salvation. He faced some of his bosses and some of his minions with something rare in the life they led, and in the home of Machiavelli no less: namely true conviction, driven not by motives of gain or envy or self-aggrandizement, but the real thing, take it or leave it. He had fallen in love with Florence, or with an idea of Florence he was not ready to betray. That they would not forgive. Just as they were about to behead him—on paper, as it's done in academia—he offered them his head on a silver plate, on which a simple inscription in elegant letters read a most inelegant *vaffanculo*.

"Candido did live to breathe free once more, and lived as he pleased, in the open ocean and on shore. But who is to say that a single episode is only an accident or a mere act of will, and not also a retrospective revelation, an obscure reiteration, the misplaced piece of a puzzle, the part of a series whose commencement, length, and final exhaustion are of an altogether different scale? It was this scale that defined his passage through Florence, and kept him in its web, whether he stayed or left. It may hold him yet.

"If the saga has a lesson, it may well be this: in the end, what triumphs is not the sublime life of the mind with all its critical fireworks—Gloria in excelsis—but *aurea mediocritas*, the humdrum mean, *le juste milieu*, the venal clutter of the everyday."

That was Mito's eulogy, as imagined by Candido, its recipient, on the day of his imagined death.

So there is another door to enter Candido's past: the very big door of the Villa. Just as for an aging racing sailor, all the races he or she ran become one race, the villa was the composite of many villas, which in Florence are dime a dozen, or rather a thousand a dozen. We could call it La Pietra, because it was so heavy, or La Trappola, because it was treacherous, but we'll call it La Gabbia, because it was in fact a guilded cage.

Let's say this villa was built in the 1480s for an agent of the Medici in France, who on his return to Florence had accumulated enough wealth to build a palatial country estate. He lived and died there. However, neither he nor his villa ever attained the resonance and prestige they aspired to. He was one of several flunkeys to the Medici, and never really made the roster of Florence's *nomenklatura* (the privileged set of people appointed by patronage to senior positions in power). He is only remembered because he paid for a fresco in the church of *Santa Trinita*, in which his face appears as a character in a religious scene. His villa—a transformed farmhouse—became one of many in the countryside.

Francesco's death, as well as the death of one of his distant followers in ownership of the property by a half millennium, are easy to reconstruct. Candido could well feign to "remember" their agonies in his imagination, for he entered the seemingly majestic villa through its big front door four years after such last demise. Candido immediately caught the scent and scenery of death—not just physical death but the death of great aspirations. Here is a past that Candido imagined, or "remembered," the moment he set foot in the palace.

EPISODE 2

In Which the First Master of a Renaissance Villa Dies in It After a Successful but Inglorious Life

Florence, 1491

Perhaps there is something that dies in every death, never to exist again; but many things return, and death itself of course, to form the vast democracy of the grave. *Ici, l'égalité.*

To make his sadness complete, worried about the draining expenses of the estate, Francesco saw his rural palace near Florence, and his fame, slip away. Like many Renaissance men, Francesco thought that a man is the son of his deeds. Now his deeds were collapsing before his sunken eyes like declining stocks.

The illustrious Francesco, one time manager for the Medici, ratified his last will and testament before his four sons. He was pleased with his description of the place: "*El palagio di grande fama et reputatione molto celebrato per Italia et altrove.*" ("The palace of great fame and reputation much celebrated in Italy and abroad.") To gain recognition, he had turned the villa, originally a fortified farm, into an ostentatious palace. Barrel vaulted corridors led into an open rectangular courtyard, whose walls were decorated with *sgraffito*, a two-toned plaster technique used on the exterior of Florentine great homes. At the back of the courtyard was an open vaulted loggia, surrounded by living quarters that had vaulted ceilings and corbels.

Upstairs were more rooms, and another open loggia, where young protégés had exercised their painterly skills.

Laden with years and fast fading glory, and memories of banking in Geneva and Lyons, the man lay dying in a vast bed with beautifully carved bedposts, which he had the servants move to his favorite room on the *piano nobile*, called the *loggia degli affreschi*. It takes no effort to evoque the lordly arches, facing east, a few steps away, and, further down, the sight of marble and fruit trees and a garden, still modest, whose stone steps led to fountains and topiaries, and into a labyrinth of boxwood.

A young man placed around one of the bedposts a garland made of laurel and lemon blossoms. He was Domenico di Tomaso di Corradi Bigordi, who people said had painted angels, *putti*, and other figures on the loggia's walls and other corridors, and festooned them with ribbons and garlands as well. Because of this obsession, they called him il Ghirlandaio. He had younger brothers, artists like himself, who painted portraits and madonnas in the busy *bottega* of the Curradi or Corradi, as they were called. He had done fine work for the Sassetti family in Santa Trinita. He had other apprentices as well, one of whom Domenico loved more than a son, like one could love an angel. The restless boy's name was Michelangiolo. Other young artists tried their hands on the villa's walls, all of them patronized by Francesco. Filippino Lippi was one of them; another was Sandrino Botticelli. After a couple of centuries, they left no visible trace. Where did their early frescoes go? Perhaps the walls were demolished, or if they were left standing, the frescoes were painted over.

The dying man murmured some verses from Dante, but soon became fatigued. Then came the revelation. Francesco looked at Domenico and the angels, and *saw* Domenico's and his own souls, and the angels' flight into the light. And he sensed that they existed in eternity and not in words or works. As for the rest, the frescoes and the palace, and the incomplete garden and the marbles, were simply things added to the universe, which he was leaving behind. This illumination brought him peace. He smiled, not minding that he was dying as little justified and as much alone as any other man or woman who has ever lived or will.

The heirs, and a few faithful domestics, rallied around the bedside of the dying man. A priest was summoned, a Mass said, and everyone in his circle of friends and relatives received the sacrament. The viaticum was administered to Francesco; and after the concluding prayer of this last office, some thought they heard him say *"in manus tuas, Dominus, commendo spiritum meum."* ("Dear Lord, in your hands I trust my soul.") He gently exhaled, and was no more. It was the year of the Lord, 1491.

In Which Two Scholars Unveil a Detailed Contract to Produce a Painting in Old Florence

The contract

Many years before, Candido met Viktor Nemirovsky in beautifully barren Terranova, where they were visiting sociologists. Viktor had, in the course of his life, pursued diverse careers. He had been a mining engineer in Siberia, but soon his interest in art, and his self-taught erudition, won him a post as curator of icons in the august Hermitage. Viktor told Candido that on a winter night, in his native long-suffering Leningrad, around the glow of a samovar, he met Kalle Kangro, a semiologist from the school of Tartu, who was also an expert on the art contracts and commissions of the Italian Renaissance. They became fast friends and wrote a monograph together, which appeared in a well-established journal. They followed the basic rules: the quoting of classics of Marxism-Leninism was required. Selection of appropriate citations became a sort of new art. Those were the requirements for every publication and public speech. The bibliographies were to start with the works of classics even though none of them had ever written anything on the subject. The best scholars, like Lazarev, Grabar, Bakushinski, Vipper, Zavadskaya, Kaptereva, Nekrasova somehow managed to publish their works in the history of art paying only a little tribute to that set of rules. The less prominent scholars like Viktor and Kalle had to pay their betters a tribute.

Marxism was the ruling dogma then, disposing their inquisitive minds to examine economics, not mainstream economics, where the doctrine of historical materialism placed unerringly the cart before the horse, but the economic aspect of noneconomic things. They corresponded with the celebrated E. H. Gombrich—a risky move— who was deeply hostile to Marxism, and who warned them about their approach. "No doubt it is interesting when studying the arts of Florence to learn about the class structure of that city, about its commerce or its religious movements," the famous gadfly told the young scholars, "but being art historians, we should not go off go on a tangent but rather learn as much as we can about the painter's craft." Officially, Kalle and Viktor of course vigorously rejected such view.

In the study of contracts between painters and patrons, Kalle and Viktor thought they found a clever compromise, and could still use Russian doctrine as a ruse. For what could be more politically correct, more proletarian, more democratic than looking at the banal, venal, and yet all-important nitty-gritty of consecrated art? Thus they discovered sociology without using that very bourgeois term. The two friends then joined a circle of reformed intellectuals in the dawning years of the Brezhnev regime, which later changed its mind about reform, harassed them, and drove them into exile. But that's a different story.

Before such auspicious mishap, Viktor and Kalle managed one time to go abroad on a research trip to Italy. They had to jump over many hoops to get permission, until it finally arrived. Otherwise, going abroad with any frequency would have implied very unpleasant things about Viktor and Kalle's connections with a certain powerful three-lettered establishment in America.

Of course, famous ballet dancers or athletes would travel abroad with regularity (although carefully chaperoned), but they brought in fame or currency. But scholars? They would have looked suspicious to the authorities of what was then called the USSR. Nevertheless, these two managed once to get permission, hoping that the official dogma would give them an ideological passport and a scientific key to enter one land and open one door that would have otherwise remained beyond their reach. In Rome and in Florence, they perused old documents and texts at the Uffizi and at the *Biblioteca Apostolica Vaticana*.

In the new world, in his America, his newfound land, Viktor told Candido the story of his life in the old world, while they hunted for mushrooms—*cantarellus* and *boletus edulis*—in a landscape whose flora bore a striking resemblance to the woods around once glittery St. Petersburg.

Candido found in Viktor's findings in Florence a subject of personal interest and intrigue. With the help of more experienced Kalle, Viktor had read several hundred formal documents recording the bare bones of the relationship from which many Renaissance paintings came, written agreements about the main contractual obligations of each party. The greater part referred to paintings that are now lost.

One agreement was between the Florentine painter Domenico Ghirlandaio and a wealthy banker of those days, whose name was Francesco Sassetti. It was the contract for a fresco in a villa referred to, in the document, as *El palagio a Montughi,*, according to some records in the old *catasto* (property record) of the city of Florence. Viktor had always harbored doubts about its alleged demolition, and suspected that the palace, instead of succumbing to the pickaxe, continued a humdrum existence under a different name. But he never followed the lead. Back in Viktor's office at Memorial University, their baskets full of plump *porcini*, Viktor and Candido examined a photostatic copy of the contract, brought in a trunk from Leningrad:

> Be it known and manifest to whoever sees
> or reads this document that, at the request of
> Messer Francesco Sassetti, lord of the manor
> at Montughi, and of Domenico di Tomaso di
> Corradi Bigordi, painter, I, Roberto di Piero
> Berardi, notary, have drawn up this document
> with my own hand as agreement contract and
> commission for a fresco to be painted by the

said Domenico in the upper loggia of Messer Francesco's manor with the agreements and stipulations stated below, namely:

That this day 12 October 1484, the said Francesco commits and entrusts to the said Domenico the painting of a fresco on the western wall of the open upper loggia, looking east; the which painting the said Domenico is to perform; and he is to color and paint angels in flight on the said wall, above figures, buildings, castles, cities, mountains, hills, plains, rocks, animals, birds, and beasts of every kind, all with his own hand (tutto di sua mano, e massime le figure) in the manner shown in a drawing on paper with those figures and in that manner shown in it, in every particular according to what Francesco thinks best; not departing from the manner and composition of the said drawing; and he must color the figures at his own expense with good colors; and he must have made the said painting within twenty months from today; and he must receive as the price for the painting as here described one hundred florins if it seems to Messer Francesco, that it is worth it; and he can go to whoever he thinks best for an opinion on its value and workmanship, and if it does not seem to him worth the stated price, he shall receive as much less as he, Francesco, thinks right, and he, Domenico, shall receive payment as follows—the said Messer Francesco must give the abovesaid Domenico five large florins every month, starting from November 1, 1484, and continuing after as is stated, every month five large florins.

And if Domenico has not completed the fresco within the abovesaid period of time, he will be liable to a penalty of fifteen large florins;

and correspondingly if Messer Francesco does not keep to the above said monthly payments, he will be liable to a penalty of the whole amount—that is, once the work is finished, he will have to pay complete and in full the balance of the sum due.

Both parties and the notary signed the contract. The contract contained themes that caught Candido's attention. (1) It specified what the painter was to paint, in this case through his commitment to an agreed drawing. (2) Neither drawing nor final painting seemingly survived, nor were there other descriptions or comments on record. (3) It was explicit about payments; it insisted on the painter using his own work and skill, and a good quality of colors; and (4) the painter and Candido had the same family name.

Candido was thrilled by the prospect that he might reside in a villa with frescoes painted by a distant ancestor—although it was possible that such place had long been demolished. He knew that his ancestors came from Mantua (where they changed their name from Corradi to Gonzaga), with branches in Liguria, Emilia, and Toscana in a forgotten past. Candido promised himself that one day, when he visited Italy again as an old man, he would do a semiserious search for his forebears in those very pretty regions, that in fact it would be fun to look at church records, enter archives, leaf through old tomes on the *araldica*—the blazoning—of his name, convinced that he would never find hard evidence, but plenty of stories to dream about a plausible past. It would be, he told himself, a retired man's little indulgence, to make good on the saying that, *comunque* ("anyway": Italy's most popular adverb), *si (se) non è vero, è ben trovato* (even if it's not true, it's well conceived). Little did he know then that, without much effort on his part, some ancestors and other ghosts would, in their peculiar fashion, and in their own sweet time, in fact reach out to him.

EPISODE 4

In Which the Last Lord of a Florentine Villa Leaves It, Decrepit but Intact, to Foreign Heirs

Florence, 1994

Fate, Jorge Luis Borges wrote, takes pleasure in repetitions, variants, and symmetries. Five centuries passed, and in the same palace, an old aristocrat lay dying on a smaller bed, and in a smaller room, which he had disposed as an intimate boudoir. Around his bed, and on the walls, were mementos of his youth: his mother's portrait, the picture of a British writer who had been a dear friend from college days (he was still in love with him), a voodoo doll, amulets, and delicate bibelots. The sounds and forms of the universe reached him wanly. He tried, in vain, to finish reading a book written by his friend Nanni Guiso. Much like Francesco five centuries before, the baron could not tell if his life's purpose had been achieved, or what that purpose was. Like Gertrude Stein on *her* deathbed (he had known her in his youth), he asked: "What is the answer? But then, what was the question?"

Over the course of the centuries, the palace, with its gardens, had seen many ups and downs, many births, and many deaths. Every few hundred years, the estate underwent necessary and unnecessary expense in pretentious renovation, when it caught the fancy and the purse of the new rich. In between, it languished in quiet desuetude, with all the features and faults of superannuated institutions: incompetence of performance, inanity, and nonentity. Throughout, it kept a tone of sadness, and felt, to those who visited its pale halls, inexplicably off. Its obscure fate was to court, unhappily, the ambition to be more, but more was always less. The makeshifts showed.

Teodoro and Federigo, Francesco's bankrupt grandsons, sold the palace to the head of a different clan in the fifteen hundreds for 3,500 florins. The deed of sale described the villa in proper Latin, as *unum palatium magnum, cum lodiis, curia, pratellis, orto, fattorio ad oleum, loco vindimie, paliis, camerij, tectis, voltis, et omnibus aliis suis pertinentibus et iuribus, situm extra et proper Fiorentiam, in populo S. Marci Veteris et in loco cui dicitur a Montughi, cui et quibus bonis confinat a primo via, a II et circum (circa) infrascripta alia bona ut infra vendita.* ("A big palace, with rooms, halls, fields, kitchen garden, oil factory, vineyard, columns, chambers, roofs, vaults, and everything pertaining to them, in and on the edge of Florence, in the domain of Saint Mark and on the site known as Montughi, all confined in their present condition to be sold as stipulated below.")

The new lord of the domain was a follower of Savonarola. His son was less evangelical, less *pazzo di Dio*, and more interested in plants. He inherited the estate. In the early sixteen hundreds, the palace passed in turn to the botanist's children. One of them became a cardinal under one of the Innocenzo Popes. He was an erudite bookworm. When Count Neri Capponi first met Candido's wife, who was related to a principal treasurer of the Holy See, he skipped the niceties of an introduction, and said directly, "Your cardinal was more important than mine. He was a banker, and mine a mere librarian." Candido could have boasted his own cardinal, Giacomo Corradi di Ferrara, appointed in 1652, but abstained. Giacomo certainly knew the Capponi cardinal before the latter died in 1659. Having a cardinal in the family is a good entrance ticket to Florentine society.

The Capponi cardinal lived in the palace for nineteen years until his death. In Florence, he spent the money made in Rome. He modified the house in the "baroque" style (in Tuscany, a tad more austere than in Rome). His architects overlaid the original structure, imposed new pediments on older lintels, and applied plaster reliefs to the ancient vaultings in the drawing room. Many years later, another member of the family became a liberal scholar of note.

When Florence was the capital of Italy, the palace served as the seat of a dour legation from the east. Florence was rapidly losing the charm of her old days, as urban developers loosed the girdle of her walls, raised ugly buildings in her ancient center, and tourists came to cheapen her sanctities. Mayor Poggi tore down the ghetto and the Mercato Vecchio, and the lament began about the disappearance of links with the past.

But the city was still charming to the foreigners that came, and every foreigner who came to Florence was "English" to the Florentines. Many of the people staying in the hillside villas were English; as were those who met at cultural centers like the Cabinet Vieusseux, or the fashionable cafés where dandies and intellectuals gathered. In the century that had just passed, many figures had spent longer or shorter periods there: Walter Savage Landor, Algernon Swinburne, Elisabeth Barret and Robert Browning, Anthony Trollope, Henry James, who wished very much to be English, and many other scions of Albion in her heyday. The palace had known some of them, and followed the times as a hillside villa for the Anglo set.

After another death, the estate changed hands and name again. During the *belle époque*, an aspiring English-speaking couple leased the place, and changed it to their taste, a modest-budget version of the Newport style of Messrs. Meade, Kim, and White. The good-looking young renter, whose wife later bought him the estate, was at the time an art dealer. His bride had fallen comfortably, and he conveniently, in love. In fact, his real love was her brother, with whom he had roomed in Paris, when they were students at the Ecole des Beaux Arts. As the years passed, the groom's convenience far outpaced the bride's initial hopeful joy. He was a cad (the illegitimate son of another cad) whose hobby was collecting, like one of Nabokov's characters, old masters and young mistresses, and in his case a few handsome *carabinieri* in between. The cad had many talents but not very large means. He followed a strong European tradition of looking matrimonially westward. She was from America, and she was rich. Unlike him, and unlike many ladies in the Florence of her days, she was not an experienced runner in the adultery stakes. She preferred to surmise and suspect, and to harbor hidden pains rather than confront directly the bisexual philanderer. To the world, she kept mum, and confided her sadness to a diary, but with little detail.

With her father's money, she eventually purchased the palace and the surrounding fields and smaller villas, as registered in the *Catasto generale Toscano.*

In the palace, two children were born. Out of wedlock, the dapper master sired at least one other child whom he well cared for but who would eventually be, through her voracious descendants, the source of endless disputes about inheritance—a story of malice and greed, and a rich pasture for lawyers in the decades to come. The younger boy died young and still obscure, although he was for a while a known fashion society painter and photographer. The older boy became notorious and lived to be very old.

For many years, this boy, later the man, traveled to distant lands—Alexandria, Istanbul, Beijing—and led a colorful gay life till he returned to his parents' home, where he was the fey prisoner of pure decorum and decor, always a stranger in accent and demeanor, and in the company he chose. Call him Rupert, Harold, or Bernie— he was one of the last members of a Proustian lineage, with literary aspirations but without issue, fond of boys, and lay now on his deathbed, laden with titles, a bit of fame, and not a few regrets. His long life had reduced him incessantly, and now that death at last appeared in full grim regalia, there was little left of him to take.

In truth, death was an anticlimax. For several years, the gentleman had been the chief mourner at his own protracted funeral, a role he had learned to accept and, as his last perversion, even to enjoy. In this, as in many other respects, he lived true to form: one of the last dandies of the belle epoque.

Through all those centuries, in such varied hands, the palace and the gardens hosted many souls. Some noble spirits vested them, but they also attracted knaves and fools. At the moment, they were almost crumbling, and the total collection of the people involved in the history yielded an unimpressive median and a middling mean of prestige. The dying baron had found in a foreign institution, an institute of higher learning, their possible salvation. Nothing, though, guaranteed firmly that his testament in the end would be deemed valid, or respected. His final stare did not rest on Domenico Corradi's angels. They had long been painted over. He once thought he had uncovered some, but alarmed at the implication if they were ever notified, had hidden them again without examining them properly. Now he stared at the window, and at the distant Tuscan skies.

Perhaps his early vision of the palace's aftermath—an elite institute devoted to idle curiosity and the mutual pollination of seasoned scholars—was slowly modified with the passing of the years. Late in life, with help from sleazy lawyers in Italy and America, he seemingly changed his mind, and was recorded supporting the presence of young students in the springtime of their prime. Perhaps he remembered his distant youth in Mighty Alma Mater, an Oxford that taught him how to teach himself, when that was all, and all was everything, and there was nothing more. Perhaps he saw the palace and the grounds on that Florentine hill as a future campus of eternal youth, where every year the flesh would be renewed, and everything that was not student life was faded ochre and ancient, gracious villas, gardens, and the shady trees, with the sole exception of a small staff, withering, like him, dismally with age. Perhaps the bright young people who filled the English gossip columns during the 1920s would return in variants and repetitions: himself and Brian Howard, along with their fashionable friends, writer Cyril Connolly and photographer Cecil Beaton. Perhaps there would be reincarnations of characters like Anthony Blanche and Ambrose Hill. Would the newcomers practice their form of revolt based on fantasy, art, elegance, defiance of manhood, and a cult of style portrayed in *Brideshead Revisited*? Or would they just jog, peck on their iPhones, and prepare for future MBAs?

In his twilight reverie, the baron could not know, nor tell right from wrong. His confessor, the old priest from San Marco, approached, and touched his hand, then administered the final rites. The minutes passed. The dying man asked the nurse for a little more oxygen, and always polite, apologized for the inconvenience he occasioned her. He breathed gratefully, then let the last breath out slowly, and gave up the ghost.

But the ghost lingered, and Candido felt its presence the moment he entered his abode, and also the presence of many more.

EPISODE 5

In Which an Art Collector, Father of the Last Lord of La Gabbia, Receives Bad News and Has an Alarming Dream

Florence, 1945

The peculiar destiny of the villa, like so many other villas, was to wallow in uncertainty. True grandeur eluded it, and utter destruction too. Instead of brilliance and tragedy, abeyance and mediocrity held sway. It expected much, and got quite little. In a dusty shelf of the upper library, a poem from decrepit Alexandria sang the Florence palace's sorry fate.

Il barone, as he was called, was actually an art dealer and collector. He was not titled, but dressed and behaved like a count—a true Edwardian gentleman, worthy of a portrait by Sargent. He thought about the palace and the poem, as he leafed through the little tome.

> What are we waiting for, assembled in the public
> square?
> The barbarians are to arrive today.
>
> Why such inaction in the senate?
> Why do the senators sit and pass no laws?
>
> Because the barbarians are to arrive today,
> What further laws can the senators pass?

34

When the barbarians come, they will make the
    laws.

Why did our emperor wake up so early,
and sit at the principal gate of the city,
on the throne, in state, wearing his crown?

Because the barbarians are to arrive today.
and the emperor waits to receive
their chief. Indeed he has prepared
to give him a scroll. Therein he engraved
many titles and names of honor.

Why have our two consuls and the praetors come
    out
today in their red, embroidered togas?
Why do they wear amethyst-studded bracelets,
and rings with brilliant, glittering emeralds?
Why are they carrying costly canes today,
superbly carved with silver and gold?

Because the barbarians are to arrive today,
and such things dazzle the barbarians.

Why don't the worthy orators come as usual
to make their speeches, to have their say?
Because the barbarians are to arrive today;
and they get bored with eloquence and orations.

Why this sudden unrest and confusion?
(How solemn their faces have become.)
Why are the streets and squares clearing quickly,
and all return to their homes, so deep in thought?

Because night is here, but the barbarians have not
    come.

Some people arrived from the frontiers,
and they said that there are no longer any
barbarians.

And now what shall become of us without any
barbarians?
Those people were a kind of solution.

The poem was written by a friend of his father, in the old, the diplomatic, the marvelous Egyptian days: a Greek from Alexandria. The baron remembered well the thick black rim of the poet's eyeglasses, the bony cheeks, the aquiline nose, the delicate hands. Constantin was his name.

In the 1940s, during the war, and the exile of its owners, the estate was quite run-down. One of the peripheral villas became a hospital. On its grounds, the Italian army built a capacious bomb shelter. It was flooded now. In the dark water still floated perhaps the corpse of a German soldier, full uniform, helmet and bones more or less intact. Not far from it, a building aboveground was disposed as a morgue. It could have been worse. Outside the estate, down the road, a different property had found a more sinister fate, and acquired a dark fame as Villa Triste. It had become the headquarters of Mussolini's goons, a paramilitary unit of torturers known, with a black sense of humor, as *la banda della Carità*. During those years, the villa remained closed, with only a skeleton staff.

When German troops occupied Florence, the main floor of the palace hosted the offices of the *kommandantur*. The estate was not kept up; the hedges were overgrown, the grass uncut. Many statues— in limestone, marble, sandstone, terracotta, cast stone, wood, plaster, travertine, and composite—crumbled. Cracks resulted from rusting soft steel armatures and pins. Scaling, flaking, spalling were in the statues found, but nothing much was damaged by the troops. The regional commander issued a diktat to his subordinates, which had, for a German, quite a delicate touch. It ordered them to leave the place in peace. Nevertheless, big guns were positioned in an area of the gardens whence they could easily blow precious central Florence, dome and all, to smithereens. Yet, gratefully, when the occupiers retreated, the Big Berthas were silently withdrawn. In his youth, the kommandant had taken courses on the history of art.

Then came the Allied troops, pushing the Germans out. They were more boisterous because they had won and caused a bit more damage than the previous invaders. But a sensible lieutenant, an art historian himself (he would be remembered as one of the Monuments Men), followed the enemy commander's footsteps, and issued his own orders to similar effect:

> Allied Military Government
> Office of the Monuments and Fine Arts Officer
> Region VIII
> September 1944
>
> TO: All units
> SUBJECT: The Villa
>
> 1. It is desired to call attention of all commanders to the fact that the above-mentioned villa is listed as a protected monument in Lists of Protected Monuments, Hq. ACC.
> 2. Under the provisions of Administrative Instruction No. 10, Headquarters Allied Armies in Italy, dated March 23, 1944, the permission of an officer not below the rank of divisional commander is required in writing to requisition a protected monument.
>
> Frederick Hartt
> Second Lt., Air Corps
> MFAA Officer

The privates were less keen. The bearded and baggy-eyed Willies and Joes, bent double under their toted weapons and glum expectations, had long been engaged in mere survival. "Just gimme a coupla aspirin. I already got a Purple Heart." The poor slobs in foxholes were now young men about town, hungry for fun. They spent their money on girls and booze. Their cigarettes they gave away, or traded them for favors of all kinds. They wanted some mementos, perhaps some amulets, and so they lobbed off the protrusions of other young men, in marble or limestone these, that flaunted their looks, their spears and their swords, their crotches and their buns, along the shaded garden paths. A finger here, a sandaled toe there, or a small cock, well proportioned, uncut. The no-hope soldiers long subjected to fatigue detail at the hands of ape-like sergeants and chickenshit lieutenants had their small revenge in the limestone private parts. At the end of the day, the penniless GIs left a penisless statuary behind.

That was what the older son of the owners found when he arrived at the villa shortly after the armistice. He wrote to his father a rather long report, quite reassuring, and promising to help in the recovery of the estate, in the new age which dawned upon the world. The family would soon be reunited, the villa restored, and fascism, after the shameful executions in Piazzale Loreto, would fade as a bad episode that once upon a time befell the brave Italians, fighters for freedom, republicans, libertarians, partisans, friends of the best in the West. The adherence to freedom and democracy was of course only skin-deep. Fascism never dies; like a coronavirus, it morphs.

When the *postino* arrived, the baron was reading a Washington dispatch stating that the United States, in agreement with France, Britain, and seven other nations, was already considering putting Italy on equal footing with other Western powers by voiding peace-treaty provisions, which branded her a defeated enemy state. Only the Russians refused to modify the Italian treaty. A servant brought a tray with an envelope on it. "*Telegramma per il Barone.*"

The news hit the dignified middle-aged recipient in the villa's upper study, at ten thirty that morning. He took it like a bullet: standing, firm chest out, the jaw determined, right through his divided, half-English, half-Italian, heart. The telegram simply said:

> Your son died last night. Heart failure. Possible overdose. Barbiturates. Awaiting coroner's report. Deep condolences. W.P. Runciman. His Majesty's high commissioner. Ferrara. September 1, 1945.

The baron could not believe his eyes. He took off his reading glasses, ready to wipe tears that, however, would not come. As he crumpled the piece of yellow paper in his right hand, his knees wobbled slightly and then he sat down. On the very large walnut table that served him as a desk were invoices from antique dealers in Dolo, in the Veneto, some photographs of sculptures he was interested in, and a few oversized art books—gifts from banks, and from publishers, awaiting his review. Suddenly, the papers danced before his eyes in wild confusion: the invoices from A. Bino Cesana in Venice, detailing the four statues sent—*spedite a Firenze*, and the fourteen *spedite a Boston, imballaggio compreso* (packaging included), the orders of brocades and velvets from Lorenzo Rubelli & Figlio— *Broccato crema, Velluto giardino, Broccatto chaudron, Raso fondo bordeaux*—the receipt of payment for *un paravent en papier gravé époque Louis XV*, sent from Paris by his friend, the *antiquaire décorateur* A. Tedeschi, who had a shop, *très mignon*, on the rue des Mathurins, the ledgers of expenses for the estate, the return of a check, non esigibile (returned) from the Bank Haskard Casardi, the second such bouncing script written by the incorrigible Mme. Keppel, a *scrittura privata* (letter of intent) for the rental of one of his other villas to the Ingegnere Perotto, and so on.

His whole life paraded as a chaotic sequence of unmanageable events. It had been raining hard outside, and now the rain was turning into a dreary sleet. He felt strictly nothing, or rather, a very large void. No stabs of sharp pain, only a muffled fear of the pain he would inflict when he told her. *That* he could not face. After very long minutes staring at the opacity of the world outside, a platoon of angry thoughts rallied in his soul.

What fool, the darling boy! Why choose that bloody shortcut, suicide? The lad had so many talents to distract him from his weaknesses. He was a consummate portraitist. His paintings were celebrated in London, and his society photographs were at least as good as Cecil Beaton's. He had a talent for collecting art, and a quick mind when it came to numbers. He, and he alone, would have managed the estate. Now everything would go one day to the elder son—a dreamer, an effete good-for-nothing, a nomad, and a flaming poof. He would let the garden go to seed, the collection slowly rot, then be sacked by dubious friends. The villa would become a hellhole of lethargic suffering. And when this heir, in turn, was gone, what then? Would the whole world that took so long to build end up in the grasping hands of an adopted heir, a gay caballero, a *chevalier d'industrie*, young, pretty, sterile and bent; or would it be a shady lawyer, or an American businessman, or a communist bureaucrat, or a simple crook, or a rapacious pimp who, in the end, would steal and soil his dream?

The baron pictured his wife and himself in free fall on the dark side of the mount they had patiently climbed, as their sole surviving son wanly waved them goodbye. This was a catastrophe bigger than the war. With these abysmal thoughts, the tired man fell asleep on the chair. His head dropped like the head of an executed man. He was visited then by a strange, narcotic reverie.

There was the noise of chatter, mixed with the sounds from a jazz quartet in the back—piano, bass, muffled trumpet, and soft brass. A crowd of well-heeled people was parading in the kitchen garden, past the fountain, past the jasmine bushes and the lemon trees, and into the ample shed where the lemons were kept during the winter. But now the lemons were outside, for it was spring, and in their stead, inside the Limonaia (lemonary,) on an improvised platform made of wood, were round tables draped in silk, with flowers and lit candles at the center. On each table, there were place settings and silver for ten. The baron heard his name invoked and, much more often, his son's, in unctuous tones—he was called "Sir this or that"—

as the milling diners spoke to, or passed, him, without knowing or caring who he was.

He soon realized there was no point in protesting, and so he played the game. They thought he was the old Marchese Della Stufa (but he knew him as a little boy!), a distant relative of the Incontri, the family who had sold him the villa, exactly one hundred years ago (for he saw the date on the program and menu printed for the occasion: May 20, 1998). My lord, that meant that he and his whole family were dead! The villa was some sort of institute, with him, and his melancholy family, the much-flattered ghosts of the weird presiding hosts.

It was a queer convocation. Some of the older dinner guests he had known as children. Many of the others he recognized only by name, because in Florence, the bodies come and go, but most names remain the same. There was a hard core of garrulous Americans who, judging from their prepossessing manner—the loud voices, the smirk of proud contentment—seemed to own the place. They were full of themselves and would soon commence their show, following a bizarre and orchestrated script, no doubt imported from abroad. They had set up a podium by the well, flanked by a superb super-woman, the wooden effigy of fertility that the baron had purchased in Dolo for the estate, surrounded by flower arrangements that were a bit too close, in his opinion, to funereal wreaths. They used an electric microphone without wires to address the assembled worthies. The dusty walls of the *stanzone* were covered with laurel leaves, supported, it would seem, by a mesh of chicken wire. *What a clever scheme*, thought the baron's ghost. To add a note of color, the green walls were accented by smaller wreaths of braided flowers and fruits, in fresh imitation of the glazed Della Robbias he had bought in 1922, or in reference, perhaps, to the mythical festoons of Ghirlandaio, often spoken of but seldom seen. The enormous room was lit by, besides the dripping candles on the tables, a profusion of Chinese paper lanterns that hung from the beams, the very same that his older son had managed to ship from Canton (today's Guangzhou), inside a huge trunk by Louis Vuitton, before the war broke out in Manchukuo. It was a glittery and dizzy mélange of themes and times, of noble silk and peasant earth, of gentle talk and some loud bursts, of elegance, vulgarity, and mirth.

The diners sat around their tables, and they were served, along with food—"No large platter, please; Americans like to be served full plates"—an endless string of speech hors d'oeuvres, from a buxom lady that rivaled the neighboring fertility goddess, not in nude rotundity but dressed in New York black and draped in a red Ferragamo scarf, who praised the late sir this or that for his gift and the dignitaries present, and the proud aristocrats, and everybody in her staff. She introduced a leader, president, and chief executive, Capo Massimo of the institute sponsoring the event, who took the mic and said the almost exact same things and then introduced her again in a perfect loop of reiterations. The turn came to introduce a member of the Board of Overseers, another man in charge of the villa (everybody speaking seemed to be in charge) and what they called "the project." The new speaker sermonized:

"I did prepare remarks, but with this darned light, I cannot read them, so I'm gonna wing it, folks. How did I come to be, of all the people on the board, the man in charge of this place? Well, our president one day looked around and asked me to do it, and in our institution, you say yes, and serve until you're fired," he said. "So here I am, for better or worse."

He got some nervous laughs.

"Let me tell ya, we've come a long way. A few years ago, other members of the board came here, took a look at the place, and saw it crumbling, didn't like it at all, and told us, 'Burn it down, and start from scratch.' The diners gasped.

"Absolutely, they told us, 'Burn it down,'" he repeated, pleased with the effect. The ghostly baron was in the back, in a blue suit, pale blue shirt, and yellow tie. He tried a smile, the Florentine aristocratic smile, the thin lips a mixture of world weariness, amusement, and faint contempt, while chewing at the same time, with the unfortunate result that a morsel of *talegio* took three steps down the palate to tap at the wrong track in the throat and nearly choked him unto embarrassed death, whence he was saved by his neighbors patting him vigorously on his back.

There was a pause full of suspense, and then a beam of reassurance shone upon the gathering.

"But our president had the vision, the clarity, and the foresight to decide that we would fix the facility so that hundreds of students could come and make the villa their headquarters and their home. And so here we are, restoring and celebrating. We've being doing this for some years already, with, as you know, our ups and downs. But we are a global institution, making the world smaller and better and safer for travel, so we will finish what we began. Our local friends in Florence decided to help, and our leader led. We salute him tonight!"

There was no salvo of salute. The applause was faint, and faded fast. Then came more introductions. A new director of the villa was trotted out. The leader explained that the director was a professor in very good and very old standing at the institution. The professor was then given a Tiffany clock, "for service," the kind given to a retiring railway man, not an incoming executive. He was on the spot now, the cordless mic thrust suddenly into his hands. He spoke softly, and promised to join two cities and two worlds,

"I belong to neither, but love them both," he improvised, "so that the villa could, one day, regain its pale glory upon the hill where it was perched." He described himself as a neutral Argentine. The baron's ghost imagined neutral Argentina, a remote country feeding the world in war and peace, open to Italian immigrants and refugees, first the Jews, then Nazis on the run, all protected by a strongman called Perón, and his blond wife, Eva. The couple had proposed sending tons of wheat to a starving Italy after the armistice. With Argentines, Italians felt very much *in famiglia*, thought the dreamer. So now, many years later, an Argentine at the villa made sense, especially if he was to mediate between Italians and Americans (but what precisely was the issue or the conflict to mediate? To whom did the villa belong? Was the ownership being contested? What, pray tell, was going on?).

To the baron, an Argentine was an Italian who spoke Spanish, dressed like an Englishman, and lived in Paris. So why not in Florence too? The new speaker was a short man, and his profile reminded the baron of a face in a fresco in Santa Trìnita: the nose and the chin were Ghirlandaio's own, insinuated and smuggled modestly among the portraits of his patrons. The director left the podium to the continuing parade.

The "project" was revealed, unveiled. The baron finally understood. The villa was a school! There would be classrooms, apartments, what they called "labs"—computer labs, language labs—and conference rooms. They would be furnished not with the existing plentiful antiques but with industrial furniture imported from New Jersey, by a firm with a glossy catalog which the men and women in charge passed proudly around, and a strange name: Ethan Allen or Ether Helen, or Elgar Heathen, or some such. Most alarming was a plan to level an entire olive grove to make room for a field of sports, a proposal by one of the university trustees. They called the future earthworks "the filling of the dale."

Shivers galloped down the baron's spine, and he thought that he would faint. More speeches followed, more presentations, special awards, salutes, thanks, praise, and finally, at long last, an invitation to walk in the gardens, under the stars, to sip coffee, and, strangely, to dance to mellow melodies in what became a jury-rigged night club. The new owners thought they had orchestrated a Tchaikovsky ballet on the villa's grounds. They produced a mixture of burlesque and *nouveau cirque* instead.

The baron reemerged from his swampy vision in stages, in a cold sweat, unsure of his ground, his life, the news, of what had happened, or would happen, to his villa. The god of wrath woke him up. He had no other reason to wake up. He was torn out like a page from a book. Outside the window, the sleet continued to come down. He discovered old fellows that had turned strange, the cypresses along the driveway. The long rows stood up as leading the way to the gates of a cemetery, the *Cimitero degli Allori*, where he was. A bird slipped past them on its way home; it was probably a crow. The statues he had bought and carefully placed now seemed lying helter-skelter in the gardens below. The books around him in the room and, above their shelves, the paintings, the old plates, his Japanese armor, the porcelain heads, the model ship, the little busts, the amphoras in terracotta seemed vulgar, ridiculous things. Now in his solitude, his *objets d'art*

failed to soothe the torn heart. Horror and fatigue were his companions. Anger too, and it was anger that helped him move to another
corner of the table, place a white sheet in the typewriter, and write:

"A questo 2 Settembre 1945, nella pienezza delle mie facoltà
mentali, dispongo quanto appresso."

He made three typographical errors. He tore the page impa-
tiently from the machine, replaced it, and started all over again in
English:

> I, (his long full name followed) being of
> sound and disposing mind and memory, do
> hereby make, publish, and declare this to be my
> last will and testament:

> First, I declare as my universal heirs my wife
> and my surviving son.

> Second, I wish that upon my death, the col-
> lection of my primitive paintings, both cataloged
> and uncataloged, and all my sculptures become
> the property of the City of Florence, and that
> they remain forever inside the villa, in via dei
> Montughi 3, site of my residence.

> Third, I dispose that both my wife and my
> son be resident custodians of the said collections
> at the villa for as long they live.

> Fourth, the income from my other proper-
> ties in Florence can be used to defray, in part, the
> costs incurred in maintaining the said villa.

He took the typescript in his hand, read and reread it several
times, and then penned, in longhand, a small postscript:

"This confirms with [sic] the arrangements made by my wife
deposited with the Avv. Mario Gobbo."

The house and the land were registered in her name, and she had made similar provisions for them, including him, and the two boys, in her will.

He wasn't sure of his English any more than he was sure of his Italian. Never mind, whoever read the will would understand. He was a practical man. He was salvaging what remained of his days and hopes from his sorrows and bad dreams.

He heard a small commotion downstairs. He looked down. Darkness reigned. The steps of several persons were bound for the upper floors. His wife had arrived in a taxi, and the servants were already disposing the boxes she had brought from downtown shops in her dressing room. He walked down the stairs with a slow, deliberate gait. His knees were failing him. His soul had long since been taken into custody. Their eyes met. This time, his were wet.

"Oh dear! Darling, you look *awful*," she said. "What is wrong?"

What the baron did not know then was that the barbarians would come one day. When that day came, Candido was among them.

EPISODE 6

In Which Candido Bigordi Is Offered a Plum Job in Florence

Tosca I

Candido was visiting his friend Mito one crisp morning in the fall. It was his last semester on academic duty, and he was savoring by anticipation the sabbatical to come, to be spent writing, and traveling by air, land, and sea. He was relishing the break from the world of scholars, tutors, and brats, especially from the manner in which the university—once a night school for dentists and accountants and lately an industrial enterprise aspiring to be a world-class research organization—was still prone to waste bright talents and overpromote the inept or corruptible, still beset by the petty rivalries between colleagues that are reflected in larger interdepartmental rivalries, and inside departments, beset by vicious fights over little spoils, like bald men fighting over a comb.

What hurt Candido the most was the realization that the halls of academe were a total washout with regards to free speech. It had long dawned on administrators and captains of knowledge that freedom of thought, including political thought, is not necessary for high levels of technological achievements and for the ability to make lots of money. So better to stick to computing and business management and a few "hard" sciences, especially at satellite campuses abroad situated in "sensitive" environments like rich medieval emirates or techno-authoritarian regimes like China. In the classroom and among colleagues, it was mandatory to have no strongly held opinion on a subject lest someone felt offended or just uncomfortable. Otherwise, he or she became a leper. In the humanities, the favored strategy to deal with strong views professed in a paper or a book was not to challenge them but to ignore the piece altogether. Silence, not reviews: neat academic omertà (in Latin America, it is called *ninguneo*). In one well-publicized instance, the administration of another school forbade an outspoken professor to interact with his peers. He was directed to come directly to the lecture hall, dispense his information to students "without bias" (like a vending machine), and go back home without discussing his views with his *chers collègues.* Some strongly objected to such treatment, but the protest was ignored.

Candido had just finished a two-year stint as dean of the graduate school, following four others as associate dean, and supervising a whole range of department at Global U. In such remit, at times he felt like a husband with forty six mothers-in-law. He would be done in January, and his wife, who worked in another division of the university (a small version of the larger caricature), had decided to resign her post in May. They were thus a few months out of phase; but in the spring, they planned to voyage together on their sailboat to shores far and unknown. In his office, Candido checked his mail on a screen and found the fateful message.

It seemed at first the offer was too good to be true, and the guarded e-mail from a senior vice president to the dean of deans, forwarded by the latter to him, intended, as she said, to feel the ground, to sound Candido as to inclinations and possibilities, implied unmistakably that, if he was interested, the post was his, almost risk-free, as acting director, and only for an academic term.

The senior officer, a highly preponderant, pushing person, large in arrangement, imperious in overture, insolent, some said, from unmerited success, unexpected, if not perverse, in attitude, and almost equally flattered and objected to in the many corridors and offices of the administration—this lady had launched her bolt quite out of the blue and had thereby made Candido ponder whether he should fear almost more than hope. In her likes and dislikes, she was equally intense, and it was her ardor, like Tosca's, that people dreaded most:

> *Fiorite, o campi immensi, palpitate*
> *Aure marine nel lunare albor,*
> *Piovete voluttà, volte stellate!*
> *Arde a Tosca folle amor!*

> Oh, wide fields, blossom! And sea winds
> throb in the moon's radiance, ah,
> rain down desire, you vaulted stars!
> Tosca burns with a mad love!

Since the early nineties, the university used the villa as a modest academic center in Florence, the umpteenth of its kind in the city, and one of several similar centers it had established in the world. This one it acquired thanks to a very generous bequest from the last lord of the domain. Every semester, undergraduate students went there to do what undergraduates do when they study abroad: learn the language, study masters and monuments, visit the sights, have a bit of foreign fun—all part of the general Californication of Tuscany. Compared with what was going on in the main campus, this was not too bad. At "home," the humanities were in terminal decline. The academic world that had helped educate Candido in Argentina and in the US, like the Argentine and the American republics where it once thrived, was befuddled and without purpose—an empty heritage that people were happy to avoid. But in Florence, the form and the content of the humanities were inescapable—death by tourism and cliché notwithstanding. An interest in high culture, the old notion that certain books and arts and forms are superior and transcendent kept alive in Florence the "reactionary" belief that students should learn to value such things before attempting their "deconstruction" and throwing them in the same heap with hip-hop. A few graduate students attended summer courses. In addition, the villa was used for meetings, conferences, and special events. It also served as a private club, and lovers' nest, for the higher echelon. Now the site was in need of a director.

The post had fallen vacant since the departure of the first appointee—a retired British diplomat, who had discharged his duties as director of the estate during the first two years following the donor's death. He left, it was said, most unhappy with the experience, and was followed in rapid succession by a series of interim administrators, of whom the reputation was that one got into trouble, and the others merely warmed their seats. The question of a new incumbent was, after such episodes, not a little pressing.

The want, thus determined, was of a person of some *gravitas*, or preferably of a united couple of some sort, of the right sort, educated and competent, a married pair having its advantage if other qualifications were marked. Professional headhunters were retained to launch a proper global search. Applicants, candidates, besiegers of the door of everyone supposed to have a voice in the matter, were already beyond counting, and the senior officers of the university had found their preference fixing itself on some person or brace of persons who had been decent and polite. Candido might have struck them as waiting in silence, though absolutely, as happened, no busybody had brought him, set to take his leave, a hint of either bliss or danger; and the notion, for the rest, seemed to have been wrought in the powerful lady and her senior executive colleagues by his record of service, and his aloofness from the many petty plots of academe. Or perhaps they just thought that he was nice and dumb, easy to handle. In any case, and in retrospect, it seems that the offer was less a compliment than a test.

It was during a long weekend in Paris, in their *pied-à-terre* on the *rue du Chemin Vert*, that the letter of offer reached them, via the Internet; it was as an alternative—or perhaps only a postponement, to research on Argentina, and a long sail around the world, that the wardenship of the villa presented itself. One semester in Florence, plenty of delicate work, ensconced in a palace, on a very large estate: Candido was offered the interim directorship of the university's branch in Tuscany (four months into the job, he would be offered the permanent post, and his spouse the coordination of the curriculum for its undergraduate part). The stipend named differed little from the modest wages at present paid them, but the interest and the prestige of the villa's halls struck them as enticing. The palace itself wouldn't be lodgings exactly, but an apartment had been carved from the old servants' quarters, under the roof. In older days, that floor seemed condemned to eternal darkness, and it housed works of art of lesser value, or so it was alleged. There would be some gain, for that matter, to their income, if ever they moved there on a fixed basis; as, obviously, though the salaries were not a change for the better, the apartment given them would make a difference, as would the free use of a car. And then there was Italy—to them as to so many, the most beautiful country on earth. But Candido's thoughts roamed a different, nonpecuniary, and non-touristic, range—his becoming familiar and intimate with the former inhabitants, who were dead but not quite gone. I shall just live with their ghosts, he thought, and my wife will commute.

The prospect seemed, for a while, rather awful. Willingly or not, they would get to know the characters that once graced those halls quite well. They might even make discoveries. And therein lay the danger, for there were "the facts," concocted or contrived by the lawyers and officials of Global U, people who asked should have.

The most peculiar shrine at which Candido was to preside— though he had always lacked occasion to approach it—figured to him as an intriguing place, a prestigious house museum, the home of a famed aesthete, the Mecca of a certain set: royals and world worthies, scholars and artists, the fey and the gay. The guests had ranged from Argentine oligarchs, Bulgarian royals, and Winston Churchill before the First World War to a garrulous and inebriated Princess Margaret after the Second. More recently, Charles and Diana had spent part of their honeymoon at the villa. When later in the year, with one of the couple in Florence and the other in New York, a stronger offer came for them to stay a full four years, it had its own unnumbered price, as it required them to surrender their impending freedom and to postpone indefinitely the peace of a yacht.

The window that had opened into a great nameless sea would close again, while another gate would open, this time into a green garden and a villa that had resonant names, that were peopled with vivid figures in a hierarchy, some of them renowned, others quite sordid, and that gave out a murmur, not of waves and wind, but one which was mixed—some of it the rustle in forest shade of all the poetry of life, some of it the hissing of vipers, and the muffled sound of unspeakable deeds.

It might seem prodigious that of this transfigured world, *they* should keep the key; but what if, instead, they were cleverly drawn into a golden cage, and ended up locked in? They pondered this, and despite it all, they thought they had a chance to make a contribution, and decided to accept. The prospect had all the excitement of a treasure hunt, but also the horror and the pity of prying open a casket that had long been shut.

In Which the Future Director of the Villa Meets a Man Who Disabuses Him of the Academic Game

The man in full

Before taking the job, Candido sought the advice of key players at the university. One of these stood out. He had heard about them but had not met any until he visited this specimen, reluctantly because he was suffering from a lingering cold.

Jack was, as in a Tom Wolfe novel, a man in full: chummy, personable, and bigger than normal, law-abiding life. In lieu of handshakes, he gave people bear hugs. He had the mien of a boxer, and the zeal of a preacher working the congregation away from the pulpit, hand clasping the cordless mic, a televangelist with dollar signs in his eyes. On such occasions, he projected affability more easily than authority. There was a jarring flippancy about a man who was asking to be king but still loved to play the fool and begged to be loved. He was charming with large crowds but bad at routine dinner-party conversation. Unless his neighbors could inspire him to talk, preferably about himself, with the future of the world as the next best thing, he mostly ignored them.

When Candido walked in his office in the university, where he was a heavyweight dean (in fact, a president in waiting), Jack was on the phone, feet on the desk.

"Look. Two and two are four. If you want it to be five, God bless you," he was telling a donor who worried that he could not manage his full pledge of seven figures over a decade, given bad economic conditions.

"I'll help you stretch the lump in the slump. We'll match it; leverage it, whatever you want. Just come see me. You know I love you, Sid."

Jack bled ego. He hung up the telephone, smiled, and recited the well-worn psalm of the showroom.

"I could sell ice to an Eskimo, and get money from a Scott." (He did not know, surprisingly, that in a university, the politically correct name for the people from the north was *Inuit*.)

"This university sells itself," he intoned. His role was that of a facilitator, making sure the Mr. Joneses and Mr. Schwartzes of this world, donors and parents, and their kids, made their decisions after a devilish pitch, and with a generous checkbook. Never mind it was a crazy, very risky world.

"Why would you wait for tomorrow to have your wish today, when tomorrow may never come?' In such style, he drove the institution like a sports car, at a fast-forward pace. Before his donors, he would sing, dance, beg, implore, and be a schnorrer to them all.

"I understand how badly somebody with lots of money wants to be somebody. This business is about honor, and prestige," he confided. "Re-cog-nition, my boy."

It was as if someone else was talking out of him. His voice had gone up one octave, hit a level, and stuck there on one didactic note. It was one of those registers you can't argue with because it just rolls on as if you are not there, so best nod him along and wait till it's run its course. It is what Candido's *chers collègues* did when they had a tête à tête with him. He let him pontificate while he thought about the man and his career.

Before delving in the law, Jack had studied philosophy and theology at Notre Dame, where his favorite teacher, himself a disciple of McTaggart, who in turn followed Hegel, argued that history was not a meaningless sequence of one damned thing after another but had a direction imposed on it by the logic of modern science, a direction that would seem to dictate a universal evolution in the direction of capitalism and liberal democracy. Though the advances made possible by science, business, and technology do not necessarily lead to political liberty, Jack thought, the human desire for recognition, cited by Hegel as the driving force of history, is best satisfied in a liberal democracy. And of all the institutions of liberal democracy, none was better suited than an entrepreneurial, private university to bestow or withhold recognition to students, alumni, donors, and to all its own variegated staffs.

In his early academic days, Jack had gotten into trouble by proposing, tongue in cheek, in the student newspaper of his *alma mater*, to launch a program of posthumous degrees. The article was titled "Retroactive Education: A Concept Whose Time Has Come." The mock proposal consisted, quite simply, of giving credits to the dead for "life experience," each credit paid with cash or plastic card, by the descendants of the posthumous student eager to upgrade their most humble, mostly immigrant, pedigrees until their forebears duly graduated, like the living and among them. It was a case of cross-generational solidarity, and it worked both ways. The scheme required minimal overhead: a secretary, an evaluating committee of trusted acolytes, a computer link to the registrar, and a dedicated account. No teachers, no classrooms, no dorms, no light and heat to pay. The aim was, as always, the talismanic folio with signatures and seals— the diploma. "A win-win situation," Jack proclaimed.

Unfortunately, what was intended as a prank was taken seriously. The piece gave rise to an acrimonious debate among colleagues, to a demonstration on campus, and to a scathing article in the *Chronicle of Higher Education*. It took Jack several years to recover from that episode, but he came back like a seasoned politician, a stronger, wiser man, and always with an eye on cash.

His office was decorated with white lilies, good liquor, baseball memorabilia, a humidor, and many photos of him with celebrities from various worlds: supreme court justices, billionaires, foreign dignitaries, the Clintons. Candido noticed there were very few books. One of them, bound in leather, was, curiously he thought, *The Higher Learning in America* by Thorstein Veblen. Jack had started as a teacher but soon found he was good in a parallel field: fundraising, schmoozing and intriguing with politicians and business leaders, attending benefits, seducing trustees. He found he was excellent at the vocation to make things grow, and his life became, basically, sales. He dreamt, and he sold dreams.

"Universities are so big," Jack told Candido, "that their chiefs become fathers, umpires, therapists, cheerleaders. They celebrate in the good times and console in the bad. We are the tireless representation of countless students, teachers, employees." Candido was not clear whether Jack was preaching or coaching him. He liked brewing strong coffee for his guests, and offered him his blend in a mug with his seal. More than a visionary, he was a modern man of spin. With him, hype sprung eternal. He liked to speak in public, although he was more the entertainer than the orator one might expect. His bloviations were an army of pompous phrases moving across the landscape in search of an idea. Once, Candido had heard him deliver his view of vision in a vibrant tone: "If we continue along the path of excellence, then, from the pinnacles of our achievements, we shall search for serendipity." He never got into his bones the essential structure of the ordinary English sentence. His metaphors left everyone confounded, and when he tried to lead from the podium, he found very few recruits to march behind a subordinate clause. After a few original deliveries of this kind, reluctantly, he let speechwriters do the trick.

Perhaps in another life, or context, Jack would have found on the stage the profession to which he had been predestined: someone who plays at being someone else, before a gathering of people who pretend to take him for that other one. In nineteenth-century America, he would have been a good performing artist on the overland trail. But in his present career, his histrionic calling gave him equal satisfaction—and equal pain. Once the last ceremony, deal, or photo opportunity ended, he needed another one, and more. To be alone with himself offstage gave him a hateful taste of unreality. What many called ambition was for him sheer compulsion. He had nowhere but up to go. If he left off being a preacher, dean, president, governor, or king of the world, he would become no one again—

his real, empty self. His secret was plain: few people were so many men as he was, and all things to all men. In him, existing, dreaming, and acting became one. Occasionally, in one of the rare moments in which he could reflect, walking in the dim light of a summer dawn on the beach, without a cell phone, before the vastness of the ocean sea, in East Hampton, he imagined an intimate affinity with a large and universal force.

"God is my morning feeling, you know." Candido tried to fathom Jack's theology from our encounter at his altar-office, to sense the whirlwind of creation, the force of growth, the sponsoring trinity of luck, bucks, and control. He pictured in his mind overworked lieutenants trying to give shape to his surprising initiatives, which he had the terrifying habit of holding before them as *faits accomplis*. To them, the great mottos of higher learning, which appeared on banners and on seals—"*veritas,*" "truth unto its innermost parts," "*per aspera ad astra,*" "*praestare et perstare,*" and so many more—must have boiled down to their leader's battle cry, taken from some popular book on cognitive-behavioral therapy: "Fake it till you make it." His was a style designed to keep middle managers on their toes, and everybody else in awe. In Jack's world, students were accepted before their dorms were built; prospective faculty were promised paradise on earth; glossy brochures, colorful websites spoke of future structures, programs, sites, in the present tense. In his book of creation, everyone began with chapter ten.

"We live in an exciting moment of change: there's a new economy, which means new institutions and new leadership styles," he explained. "The new corporations are a corporate mirage created to make lots of money fast, and based on debt. Derivatives and poetry all in one. New institutions of higher learning are quite similar. We, new leaders of this world, are more concerned with managing the image, the prestige, the stock price, or the country risk, and profiting from it, than with running real companies, real universities, real governments and states. Look at this place: poor classrooms, low salaries, little space; but this is a sleepless, booming, sexy American city where everybody wants to be, and we got great press. The applications and the donations grow and grow."

"But what if there's no fit between the mirage and old-fashioned reality?" I dared to ask.

"Reality, my friend, had better catch up, or there'll be a lot of sorry sad sacks left holding the bag one day. If the new-world plane crashes, we'll make sure to keep the few parachutes on board to ourselves, and bail out just in time. If I were president of the United States, I would pardon myself before leaving the scene."

"Speaking of boards, aren't your trustees concerned? Don't they control?"

"Boards are like sweethearts to a smart leader. You always keep in touch with them, consult, ask, but mostly tell them what they want to hear, and give them only good news. You must pamper them, spoil them, and give them simple figures, climbing charts. It is all about fundraising and love, a lot of hand-holding, charm, charisma, and *mano a mano*," he intoned. He also winked. "You should try to form a board to run you, so you can run the estate by running them," he added.

"Jack, you've just given away duh secret of duh trade, it seems."

"That's the way it is, my boy. Do not feel discouraged by your new job. It's a great challenge. Get in shape, take a big breath, and run with the bit," was his advice. "In my mind, failure is never a consideration," he said in tones reminiscent of Maggie Thatcher before the Falklands War. "Do not wait for instructions, permissions, and permits. Just get a broad go-ahead signal, then be bold. Seize the day. Before long, voilà—it's a *fait accompli!*"

"I'll make enemies."

"Who does not? Mine give me energy. They hate me, and I welcome their hatred. Do not always keep an eye on your competitors or your nominal bosses. In my case, only rivals from another era win my admiration: Napoleon, Winston Churchill, Robert Moses, and Tricky Dick. I study their courses and race against them. But don't wait long to get a board to oversee you. It's much safer than having a boss. When your initiatives succeed, when you perform a stunning *fait accompli*, a board will crown you, but a boss will get rid of you."

If Candido had needed a shot in the arm, then Jack gave him a full broadside. The man was fearless. In lieu of an adieu, he simply said: "We are all worms. But I do believe that some of us are glow-worms." When Candido left Jack's office, his chest had expanded, his wheezing had stopped, and, for the first time in months, he breathed a deep, luscious, full-polluted breath of New York air—an air you can trust because you see it; the same air that fattened Donald Trump.

On his way to the top, Jack gave unhealthy advice, and none of what he envisioned turned out well: not for the villa, not for Candido and his wife, and after a meteoric rise, not even for him, who was eventually and unceremoniously booted by his board of trustees after the entire faculty turned against his rule in a coordinated fit of resentment, called a nonbinding vote of no confidence.

EPISODE 8

In Which Candido First Becomes Acquainted with the Villa

It looked most impressive when they first went. As soon as they were announced, the gates to the estate opened slowly, automatically, as in a version of the *The Wizard of Oz*. A straight, majestic alley, bordered by cypresses and stone, seven hundred yards long, led to another open gate, flanked by statues, past a moat. A rotunda of sculpted yew, with a Roman basin in its middle, was brilliantly positioned in lieu of a forecourt, so as to deflect oncoming forces from the long line of approach. The road, Candido thought, called for a vintage Rolls conveying a monarch, reigning or deposed.

The villa stood big and square on a softly rising hill. It was curiously grand, stiff, sunny outdoors and gloomy inside, musty, austere, and ostentatious all at the same time, like one of those palaces built by writers to suit a murder mystery, or a gothic tale. It had all the rich ingredients—the atmosphere, the *genius loci* once sedulously searched by the *anglo-beceri*, as the English (and some American) expats in Florence were called, and reproduced in the Merchant Ivory films: cultivated fields, formal gardens, a chapel, an expanse of shuttered windows, a murky past with many stories, sixty rooms that witnessed boredom, domestic and illicit love, conversations about art, history, and theft. The world of the *anglo-beceri* was very proper in facade. It was inhabited mainly by wealthy expatriates and members of the old Italian aristocracy—a set of people who spent their days visiting one another's exquisitely refined gardens and crumbling villas on the hills of Florence and getting into interminable philosophical disquisitions. Some people told Candido that in the past, this villa had also languished in propriety, but others thought that it had rocked with fuck.

They had never been inside before. Candido and his wife, Maria Cunegonde, arrived by taxi from the train station, Santa Maria Novella, on a dim winter day that followed the *befana*. They were greeted by a skewer of characters lined up in the direction of the massive wooden doors, and long familiar to the place: a lawyer (awkwardly dressed in a suit that did not fit), an accountant, a secretary, the head gardener, two cleaning ladies, an armed guard. To picture this, think of Downton Abbey poorly staged. The greetings were ceremonious: all smiles that a few pairs of squinting eyes betrayed. The couple was total strangers but no ordinary visitors, since Candido was meant to administer the affairs and the interests of the institution that was heir to the estate. They paraded past the line. Presentations were made: *IL nuovo direttore e la sua moglie.* The luggage was lugged. They were shown four rooms on the top floor.

Com'è duro calle lo scendere e'l salir per l'altrui scale. (How sad a path it is to climb and descend another's stairs. Dante—*Paradise.* XVII. 58. 9) The coming two years would give a quite literal meaning to Dante's words. They were then given a tour.

In the dim light, it seemed a very large and handsome palace, a bit on its heels. Past a *T* of corridors, through a grand oval antechamber, dressed by marble stairs that flowed to a side, they walked from one room to the next: the *salone*, the dining room, the old studio and the *studiolo*, the library, the corridors, a sequence of parlors, a fanciful bathroom. Upstairs, they saw bedroom after bedroom, more antechambers, and the grand ballroom with a shiny crafted parquet floor, chairs lined against the walls, and up above, a screened balcony for an orchestra to sound unseen.

It was an uncanny sort of place, as if under a spell. The walls were red, off-white, pale ochre, green, and blue. Damask covered many, especially the rooms where art was prominently displayed. The oriental rugs were threadbare, and so were the tapestries hanging in some halls. The closets in the changing rooms (we dared open some) were packed with gowns. Of those, many were Chinese. But the vast collection of ladies' shoes and hats made the place seem the treasure room of a lady shopper in the Paris of the belle epoque who found some of what she wanted at Doucet's, and the rest only a few steps farther, at Worth's, at Paquin's, or at Raudnitz's: the loot from a successful shopping spree at the Rue de la Paix. It was all so still and quiet, giving the impression of a lived house where the owners had lapsed into an eternal nap. A spiritual dimension emerged from the bric-a-brac of decades dedicated to collecting art and "stuff." A lifetime had been spent to turn the villa into a single cabinet of curiosities. It was the last surviving palace of a grand tour, which once spanned half the globe, from the fields of Italy to the world's silk routes. And Candido was supposed to preside over its restoration! Was he a savior or an executioner? Candido recalled Stefan Zweig's requiem for a hotel in Zurich which became a tax office: "With the vanishing of residences of this kind, a significant portion of the town's soul also vanishes and what one generation sees painlessly depart, a few years later will prove a grievous loss to the next."

The overall effect was more *nature morte* than normal life. The spaces were dead, no longer breathing at all. The scent of the bygone came from the mold behind the broken damask on the walls. In those rooms, an art dealer, a lesser contemporary of Stibbert, Berenson, Bardini, and Horne, had managed to compose an atmosphere of openness to the culture and religion of the *duecento* and the *trecento*, with added chinoiserie by his son, not only through the objects they collected, but especially through the manner in which they placed them, often forcing strange alliances between periods and places, between the sacred and the profane, between the genuine and the fake, between the sublime, the naive, and the merely kitsch. Candido took an instant liking to the library—an eclectic collection of fine leather-bound tomes. There, alone on a rectangular piece of furniture, at the end of an imaginary runway marked by three billiard lamps which hovered above a long walnut desk, sat a faded polychrome Buddha, as if waiting for a yellow-robed priest to chant his evensong.

The place was a gentle wreck—not like an automobile or an airplane wreck, but more like the hull of an old ship abandoned on a beach. Like for Stefano Benazzo, the photographer of shipwrecks, for the newcomers, this wreck was an image of peace and serenity. It invited them to imagine the experiences, the fears, and the dreams of so many people whose lives had passed.

They had the sensation that a large orchestra of ghosts was in the shadow, which played a strange music that nobody could hear anymore. Every space had the same sense under their breath, as if something was going to happen, but nothing happened at all. The more they breathed, the more the oxygen felt scarce. Years of dead air; so many, that the count was lost. Only a muted conversation took place between the various rooms. Ghosts came and went, walking with felted steps, talking in soft tones. (They soon learnt from a logbook that a guard on watch had left in a panic, claiming to have heard, late at night, *passi felpati*.) In due course, they would learn to be their friends. The ghosts felt threatened but posed no threat. At most, they were capable of pranks to tease the invaders.

They spent the first night in the cavernous bedroom in the apartment they had been assigned, on top of the other floors with nobler rooms. The little window high above offered no view of the outside. It was chilly, lonesome, and sad. When they woke up, they were startled to find, at the foot of the bed, an offering meant to protect them: a little medal of the Virgin, surrounded by a circle of crumpled silver papers. They took it as a message from spirits that felt a kindred sympathy for them.

In one of his short stories, published in the volume *Tit for Tat*, Harold Acton portrayed a villa like this where Candido and Maria now slept. He chose to name it *La Trappola*. The tribute of the medal was more a kindness than a warning from all of them: the families that came before—nobles of Florence—who first designed the villa as a pretentious farm and pleasure-house. It was the new couple's turn to live in the palace. Had the bygones felt similarly trapped? They did not know—only suspected that the spirits were trying to communicate. By the next day, one thing they did surmise. Since the last lord died, the villa was laid siege not by its phantoms but by modern hordes, which descended upon her announced or unannounced, on schedule or by surprise, and always in force. The estate was haunted by the living, and its ghosts were in bad straits.

The morning brought bright light, different vistas, and new hopes. Candido and Maria ambled in the garden, which seemed composed of a series of roofless rooms divided by high hedges, cascading slowly down the hill. It was a masterpiece of design, in its variety, in its balance, in its *feng shui*, in its steadfast commitment to the color green, not just one but several greens: pine-needle green, ilex green, boxwood green, the green of bay leaf and the green of yew.

In its present form, the garden was the decaying legacy of local and foreign designers—Italian, Polish, British, and American. The garden was an extension of the house yet a space in its own right. As in other Tuscan villas, it was a back garden, which one visits after having been admitted to the private domain of the house. The design coaxed the viewer to walk down and also to look ahead. The gaze and the body were invited to move along a curve following the clock: the back against the wall; to the left, tall trees; ahead, two fountains on a line, down a slope. The plot farthest away from the home ended with a pergola, then a tall hedge; beyond, a dale, the distant city, some hills, and the sky. As one descended the garden steps, from one fountain to the next, to the right and to the left, avenues of lawn lead to yet other enclosures, square, oval, and round. Here and there, statues in marble, cement, and sandstone presided, reminded, and suggested to the literate the feats and feasts of a baroque mythology. Their bodies were a frozen festival of calves and buns, spotted by lichen and tanned with moss. In such a garden, one wanted to stay and also longed to fly, transported by dreams. What had the garden seen, and what would it witness again?

SEASON 2
The Inmates

Angels in Italia

EPISODE 9

In Which Candido Meets One Ghost

The firefly

July in Florence can be an experience of suffocation. The air does not move. It is hot, humid, and there is smog. The evening brings some relief. At the villa, upstairs, Candido tried to read, but it was disquietly warm. With windows open, in hope that a gentle breeze might come down from the hills up north, he heard the frogs singing in the fountains, and saw the intermittent blink of the fireflies. One of them meandered in, as if in synchrony with the page of Harold Acton's memoirs open on his lap. Acton described scenes of his childhood in a villa not far from the one that currently imprisons him. Candido read:

> In the green dusk a ragged bat or two zig-zagged low with a shrill twitter, and glow-worms lit up aquarium depths of aromatic herbs. A sudden rush of ideas that seemed altogether new, a crystalline alacrity of mind, was fanned by the evening breeze: the mellow walls absorbed one's secrets and the marble busts smiled down benevolently.

Then torpor swamped him. The ambient light was dim. The wandering glowworm posed itself on an armchair. And all at once, that spark caused a wonderful conflagration to spread in Candido's morose mind. The little light went off and then it lit up again, this time shedding a larger glow, as if enveloped by gauze—a spectral light, the shimmer of a ghost. Candido had expected something of the sort. Then it spoke. Could it be her? It was, and she spoke.

"*Perchè Lei non fa finta di agire, senza agire?* They put you in charge, but won't let you do? I think it's better not to do anything about this place: let it fade, let it rot. I used to think I loved it, and perhaps I did, but not after the war."

"But, Signora, I fear that unless I am allowed to do what's proper for the villa, it will become something hideous, a contraption..."

"*Un machin eh?*"

"*Oui, un machin.*"

"Perhaps you are right. Besides, I don't get the feeling that you like being a hack, a hapless soul."

"Not at all. I would find that demeaning, and a hellish waste of time, even in a grand place."

"The villa will be defaced by restoration, no matter how good."

"If you could only see how grand we made it, my husband and I. Fancy-dress balls and *tableaux vivants* were then the fashion. In Villa Schifanoia—"

"Oh yes. The European University should take better care of it."

"A ball was held combining Persian and Venetian costumes. My husband and I were dressed in clothes designed from Persian miniatures. We hosted a few of these events in our *teatro verde.*"

"I've seen the old pictures."

"Aren't they swell? We managed to reproduce the color, and watched them in 3D!"

"You are a bit like them, right now."

"Like them, I'm a shimmer of what was, and I am not. You must think you are dreaming. Let me tell you something odd: I'm dreaming *you.* One day you'll understand."

"I won't even try right now. I just let this be."

"Are you afraid?"

"No. I am intrigued. You are attractive, and there is fire in your eyes. I seem to remember those eyes, that fire, as if in a distant past, we had shared other dreams... *Amarcord*... Did we know each other in some warp of time? Did we fall in love?"

"Remember? It was siesta time, a summer or two before the Great War: a young mother languished under the linen sheets, wished her husband would come and hug her there and then, but no, she knew the bastard had tiptoed from his study, where he pretended to work, up the secret spiral stairs to the servants' quarters and fallen into the arms of one of the maids, to sire more little bastards under the very roof that housed his legitimate wife and their two sons."

Now, as she was falling asleep, burning with lonely pain and desire, she saw a golden boy, a winged adolescent, burst through the bedroom wall, rip the damask that covered the old frescoes, and come into bed with her, to enact every verse of the book she had been reading:

> Twice or thrice had I lov'd thee,
> Love must not be, but take a body too;
> And therefore what thou wert, and who,
> I bid Love ask, and now
> That it assume thy body, I allow,
> And fix itself in thy lip, eye, and brow.
> Whilst thus to ballast love I thought,
> And so more steadily to have gone,
> With wares which would sink admiration,
> I saw I had love's pinnace overfraught;
> Ev'ry thy hair for love to work upon
> Is much too much, some fitter must be sought;
> For, nor in nothing, nor in things
> Extreme, and scatt'ring bright, can love inhere;
> Then, as an angel, face, and wings
> Of air, not pure as it, yet pure, doth wear,
> So thy love may be my love's sphere;
> Just such disparity
> As is "twixt air and angels' purity"
> Before I knew thy face or name;
> So in a voice, so in a shapeless flame

> Angels affect us oft, and worshipp'd be;
> Still when, to where thou wert, I came.
> Some lovely glorious nothing I did see.
> But since my soul, whose child love is,
> Takes limbs of flesh, and else could nothing do,
> More subtle than the parent is.
> "Twixt women's love, and men's, will ever be."

"I do remember. Ethereal love, but very intense. But how can *you* remember?"

"I told you, in some warp of time."

"Oh yes, while upstairs, above your bed, your husband acted out another, racier verse… Let's say I imagine, not remember."

"From the same poet, could that poem be, which could apply to he who cuckolded me."

"Of course, look at this other page from Donne:

> Come, madam, come, all rest my powers defy;
> Until I labour, I in labour lie.
> The foe ofttimes, having the foe in sight,
> Is tired with standing, though he never fight.
> Off with that girdle, like heaven's zone glittering,
> But a far fairer world encompassing.
> Unpin that spangled breast-plate, which you wear,
> That th' eyes of busy fools may be stopp'd there.
> Unlace yourself, for that harmonious chime
> Tells me from you that now it is bed-time.
> Off with that happy busk, which I envy,
> That still can be, and still can stand so nigh.
> Your gown going off such beauteous state reveals,
> As when from flowery meads th' hill's shadow steals.
> Off with your wiry coronet, and show
> The hairy diadems which on you do grow.
> Off with your hose and shoes; then softly tread
> In this love's hallow'd temple, this soft bed.
> In such white robes heaven's angels used to be

Revealed to men; thou, angel, bring'st with thee
A heaven-like Mahomet's paradise; and though
Ill spirits walk in white, we easily know
By this these angels from an evil sprite;
Those set our hairs, but these our flesh upright.
Licence my roving hands, and let them go
Before, behind, between, above, below.
O, my America, my Newfoundland,
My kingdom, safest when with one man mann'd,
My mine of precious stones, my empery;
How am I blest in thus discovering thee!
To enter in these bonds, is to be free;
Then, where my hand is set, my soul shall be.
Full nakedness! All joys are due to thee;
As souls unbodied, bodies unclothed must be
To taste whole joys. Gems which you women use
Are like Atlanta's ball cast in men's views;
That, when a fool's eye lighteth on a gem,
His earthly soul might court that, not them.
Like pictures, or like books' gay coverings made
For laymen, are all women thus array'd.
Themselves are only mystic books, which we
—Whom their imputed grace will dignify—
Must see reveal'd. Then, since that I may know,
As liberally as to thy midwife show
Thyself; cast all, yea, this white linen hence;
There is no penance due to innocence:
To teach thee, I am naked first; why then,
What needst thou have more covering than a man?"

"We seem to know our Donne quite well."
"A poet of love."
"And witty soft porn."
"Now let me tell you what I told nobody, ever, but which you
managed to guess. The angel stretched beside me and kissed me—a
kiss that, as I tried to object, gagged my voice while his arms tight-

ened round me, straitjacketing my body. His action revealed a divine creature, irresistible and shameless. My piety had limits… I fought faintly and then let myself go in a delirious abandon. The immense room moved above and about me, in wild gyrations, as I felt the stiffness of his shaft, announced by a mindless smiling head, burrowing a path in the velvet sheath of my sex. The photographs of my parents and grandparents (you have seen them downstairs as I left them), in their elaborate silver frames, seemed aghast to see my virtue heaving in waves, like an ocean, under the thrusts of a winged stallion. And I began to feel happy. It was my turn then. I hugged my boy, embraced him, kissed him. "My child, my Cupid," I whispered, "you who are all my power, you who are my arms, my hands, my magic, bend your bow, my darling, and sink your shaft, which never missed a challenge, into the heart of my sorrow." And he did, while I groaned and fainted in bliss, and then he vanished, leaving me to wake, an hour later, from a delight that I would keep henceforth in my bosom, as my secret reverie."

"Your airy angel, dear Signora, was more attractive than your hairy priapic husband, and you are infinitely preferable to that besotted maid he pinned in the laundry room."

"So sweet she feigned to be, so docile. To think that she breastfed my two sons when I failed to give them my own milk. Oh, *perfida puttana*… But don't flirt with an old lady, sir. How could you possibly know such things? You even seem familiar with my avenging angel, whom you could have dismissed as a figment of an unhappy wife's imagination."

"He is a figment of my imagination too. I feel like a father to that creature, or myself a winged stallion in my youth. As for your husband's trysts, they were notorious in Florence, and not just with the ladies. He liked to be impaled from time to time by robust men. Everybody spoke of him as a *donnaiolo*. Besides, it does not take much to figure that a cad's frequent infidelities are so many reminders to his wife that she possessed neither the piquant flavor of a mistress nor the artistic talents of a rightful citizen in his collector's world, and that all she had to offer was her money, upon which he graciously consented to live. And as for flirting with an old lady, madam, people who share a present are forever sharing the moment. There is no age. Whatever we have been, or are, we should let without further question be."

"Now *you* are talking like a ghost."

"We share this moment. Let us make the best of it."

"We share a predicament; we are trapped between these walls. You cannot get out before notifying the guard downstairs. He will then turn off one or two alarms before you can take even a small walk in the gardens with your dog. I know the feeling. In my days, we had the servants inside, and outside at night, the guard dogs. I too was always watched."

"I just read an account of Florentine prisons in the 1780s. In the *Stinche,* there were five doors to pass before one came to the courtyard. The opening of the first was three feet wide, and four feet nine inches high, with a sad inscription over it, I forgot. The chaplain had apartments, and resided in the gaol. I feel like him."

"I know the feeling. When my husband died, my son and I were left alone in the villa, not really living but leading an afterlife. We were ghosts already, in his case because he had a sexual secret, and in my case because of the brutal war that fell upon the villa for the second time. Upstairs, in one of the trunks in the attic—the Louis Vuitton ones—you may find my diary of those days."

"*Oportet misereri.* The words came from the wall, behind a dull Seicento portrait of an English lad."

"What was that voice?"

"I've heard it before. Don't be alarmed, sir; it's the Gran Duca Pietro Leopoldo. He visited the villa several times in the convulsed 1780s to take a rest. He was an honest ruler but a bit of a bore. Austrian, you know… Loved speaking Latin, using spies, and keeping notes. He constantly moved to check on his subjects. His portrait downstairs does not flatter him, nor does his wife's. They are portraits of *lèse majesté!* My husband said whoever painted them should have been shot. I see them every day, from my own portrait, above the desk of that obsequious receptionist (a vicious little spy, by the way). Poor couple. And for *sua Altezza Reale,* what offense! To think he was the brother of beautiful Marie Antoinette. *You* should read his memorandum on the Tuscans: it will help."

"Good grist for my profession?"

"Exactly. 'Sociology,' you call it? Much practiced in Chicago when I was young, mostly by ministers' sons. If they were bright at all, they finished their studies in Germany, then came back to teach at the university. One of my distant relatives taught the subject in Chicago. He was a Norwegian humorist, a self-taught polymath, ready to denounce the America of the newly rich. His name was Thorstein Veblen, but we called him uncle Thor. He savaged the Rockefeller-funded university that hired him, and ran away with the president's wife! He was dismissed, of course. But here, in Palazzo Pitti, the Tuscans had their very own sociologist long before somebody gave your profession that mongrel name and humdrum destiny. He was a foreigner like you and I, and a philosopher king! I once owned a reedition of Pietro Leopoldo's book. It's called *Relazioni sul governo della Toscana*. The man goes straight to the point. I had occasion to revisit his notes after I was put in jail."

"But you, cara Signora, got out."

"Yes! Angry and relieved, and from two jails at once: the woman's prison and the villa. I thought then that it was for good, but I was wrong. I came back, lived and died as a recluse in the villa, and here I am, with a pile of things left undone, talking to you, who will dismiss all this when you wake up."

EPISODE 10

In Which the Ghost Shares
Her Sorrow in Florence

The diary

"Will you tell me about your imprisonments and disaffections, Signora?"

"Gladly, I'll use my diary as a guide, but first, you must make yourself a drink. I like to watch."

"Will bourbon do?"

"Your choice. I preferred martinis in my day, extra dry, with a twist. But, as you can imagine, I'm a teetotaler now."

There was a pause. I went to the kitchen to get some ice, and then poured myself a full jigger of Maker's Mark.

"This may be interesting. It was in June 1940, at the beginning of the war."

She brightened up.

"Springtime for Hitler, and for Mussolini too. Despite the season, in Florence, I felt cold. It was such an incredible and unexpected experience."

"My husband wanted to remain in Florence to look after the villa and garden as they were his passion and his lifework, but I felt the Fascists would be very vindictive and dangerous. I also wanted to be in touch with the boys, so I tried to get a Swiss visa. Everyone said, 'How foolish. You will be far more comfortable here; no one would ever disturb *you*. *You* are looked upon as one of *ourselves*.'"

"However, I did my best to get a visa. Italy declared war on June 10. I had a luncheon that day, but the duce only announced it at six o'clock in the evening, and they went in on Tuesday, the eleventh. Thursday, the Torrigianis came to tea still *insisting* on our staying here. The boys could write us. That day, I was expecting Mme. Maccaferri and Olga Kondacheff for tea, when at 4:20 p.m., two officials were announced—wanted me to go to the *commissariato* at once to answer some questions. I said people are coming for tea, but they said it would not take long. They had a car at the gate, then picked up my husband who was at Villa Sofia *with the Podesta,* who said he would telephone and make it all right!

"They drove me directly to the woman's criminal prison. My husband said, "This looks bad—it is like a prison."

I laughed and said, "Why should they put *me* in prison?" But a Jewess wife of a Polish Jew was also there and told me this was in retaliation for England taking some Italian waiters to prison! And in London, prisons are palaces compared to those in Italy. Of course, *as Jews,* these Landaus got out immediately—also strange! Then Mrs. Caccia joined us—it really seemed a joke. We took it like that, never dreaming we should be kept for twenty-four hours.

"That was Friday, June 14. Mrs. Caccia was taken to the *questura* just at lunchtime, so she had no lunch. Finally, after sitting about waiting in vain to be liberated, we were sent upstairs to find a place for the night. This was called the 'Nido' as children were kept there—a room for nineteen horrible birds. I refused to lie down but sat in a straw chair in the corridor, my feet on another. Mrs. Caccia had what they called a 'comfortable' chair upholstered, but I was afraid of it. I was very cold having a thin gown—no coat. So when Mrs. Caccia was liberated at 12:30 p.m., I took her chair, which was better, though hard as a rock. Of course, sleep was out of the question, and I was very cold. Naturally, we were locked in. I had a light lunch but did not think of eating anything.

"In the morning, after the longest night I had ever spent, I found they gave absolutely nothing but boiling milk! I told the nun I could not drink milk, but she refused even a crust of bread. However, later we were taken to the refectory and given bread and cherries.

One paid for everything except bread. We were locked out in court-yard while they cleaned the rooms. Miss Ballard—a young girl who had been to the villa—came up and spoke. She was in a cell of ten sleeping on the floor on a straw sack. At midday, we had a meal. I could eat only a crust of bread and a tiny cheese in tinfoil. I asked for a cup for wine. There were no more cups, but I asked if they could send out and buy one? No. But I had not had a drop to drink for twenty-four hours. The nun was helpless, could suggest nothing. But fortunately the servant—a girl put in for abortion—offered me her cup, which I was glad to accept, and had some acid wine. The smell of the food was disgusting, served from pails in deep tin things like a *pot de chambre* without a handle—greasy and smelly, with fork and spoon of wood mostly old, black, and, of course, filthy. How any of these women could eat anything, I could not understand. We could not have cherries again without taking the whole 'pranzo.' They took our money away when we arrived and charged what we ate to our accounts, which was very confusing as the nuns were not accustomed to this sort of thing. There was only one meal a day. Bread and milk in the morning and bread at night.

"I expected to be liberated any minute. Some women there were very old, and a girl whose lover was a friend of one of the big men in Rome told me surely some of my friends must know a 'pezzo grosso' in Rome! More English kept coming in. All ages though sixty-five years was the limit in England. Nobody came for me, to my amazement. I could not believe they would treat my husband and me so, nor could any of the people there understand it.

"Another night passed cold and sleepless. My maid had sent me a suitcase, but I had no place to put anything. My chair was at the end of the corridor, so I only took out the coat and left it in *deposito*. The nights were so cold my coat did not keep me warm, but someone lent me her dressing gown to put over me, which helped. I never took off anything but my hat. We had nothing to do—were locked out in the dismal courtyard while they were cleaning—more or less, but one was glad to be in again. The hours dragged. Nothing happened, and I felt as though I had always been there, and always should be.

"How the day passed, I don't know. Mrs. Ballard had got her young daughters out as she was an American separated from her English husband, and in charge of her daughter who was under-age. In the morning, I was told my husband was out, which was a great relief. In the afternoon, Mrs. Ballard came to see me, bringing me some things. No food was allowed. She said my husband said I was over sixty-five—had changed my passport years ago—but he could not prove it. As I had even my handbag ready packed to go to Switzerland and had our marriage certificate in it. I told her he could find it in the bag in the safe.

"About six o'clock, I was told I was free! I asked if they could telephone for a taxi. No. I could walk, so I took my useless heavy bag and walked over two squares where I found one. My husband had come for me, but they said I had gone, or would not give the message. When I got home, I found we had been in luxury compared to his place. He was with ten men in a small room, sacks on the floor with some knotted stuff in them. The *filthy* food he could not touch in dog bowls on the floor. Water also in terracotta bowls—new—with oil and straw floating on the water. In the corner was a wooden pail for *all* necessities! When he asked for a latrine, the hateful warder said there was none.

"We had a toilet we could not lock—dirty and leaky—and when I asked for paper, there was none! Fortunately, I had a little in my bag, and a disagreeable woman came to take our messages for what we wanted, so that was all I asked for. My only fear was that for lack of food and sleep, I should get ill and be taken to a hospital. I certainly could not have stood many days like that.

"From the day I got out, I had not even *a line* from anyone but a kind woman, who also sent me flowers, also a Hungarian woman. And twice, *one* real friend telephoned, wanting to come see me, but I sent word I would let her know, as I did not want her to get in trouble. After I left, I had a souvenir sent her. Those who were so anxious I should stay never noticed my existence, nor anyone else but a good soul or two.

"Predictably, of course."

The booming voice of Pietro Leopoldo behind the picture again. And he said, as if proud of his accented Italian,

"Nella Toscana sono continue e frequenti le mancanze contro la buona fede, le truffe, gl'inganni nei contratti, le falsità e tutte quelle specie di delitti provenienti dall'inganno, dall'interesse e mala fede e che esigono talento, furberia ed accortezza, ma non coraggio."

("In Tuscany one finds frequent breaches of good faith, chicaneries, fraud in contracts, lies, and all manner of crimes related to deception, venal interests, and bad faith which require talent, cunning, and sagacity, but never courage.")

"How true, how true! I felt it then, *in carne propria*."

She continued.

"The next day, I spent most of the morning waiting about frustrated. Then when my husband had gone to the bank, the sirens shrieked. And no one being allowed in the streets, I had to go into the bank. A farce, I thought—no one wanted to bombard Florence. At 2:30 p.m., I went to the Swiss Consulate and got my visa. I then got tickets, then Maria, the maid, took trunks and bags to be examined and recorded at the *dogana*. They were most polite. Coming downstairs of the consulate, I missed the last step and hurt my foot. I went home and put on a bandage with Eau de Goulard. One friend came to tea. I dined at seven o'clock, though I had no appetite. I was so glad at the thought of getting away from a place where everyone was so terrified they dared not even send a card of sympathy. I could not understand such cowardice. One man sent me flowers, also one woman who was no friend. Only one had twice telephoned wanting to come see me, but they would not let her. Our telephone was tapped.

"The following day, I was up at four in the morning, left with Maria at five forty. The train was packed—I had to go second class to Milan. Fortunately, it was very cool. We arrived at ten thirty and went to Gallia for lunch at noon—not a soul there. At two, we left for Domodossola—an empty train. It poured all afternoon. We arrived at 4:16 p.m., Italian time, so had to wait an hour, but soon got in a delightful huge carriage all alone. I left Maria, who went back to Florence. It poured, so one could not see the lovely country well.

But oh, the heavenly sense of freedom when I got across the frontier! From a hell of uncertainty to a heaven of security. I only felt anxious about my husband and the boys, though I hoped to hear from them soon. Also it was appalling to think of the poor creatures still in S. Verdiana and the Murate. At 8:02 p.m., I arrived and found only forty people in the hotel, so I got a nice room. I dined in my room and took veronal. The trunks came the next day.

"In Switzerland, I read the *shameful* conditions of the armistice. French treachery was at play. But what now? Could anything be done? Hitler said every village in England would be in flames soon. Life would really not be worth living—not possibly in Europe.

"My brother wrote me from Chicago. 'How could you possibly go back to Florence again?' Well, as you know, I did. So much would happen, so much would change, for better and worse."

"I'm very thankful and moved, ma'am, for confiding all such sadness in me, and honored too. It was an unusually long speech for spectral tradition."

"*Maledetti Toscani.* I've kept it in my chest for all these years. I had only trusted the story to my diary, before I told you. Now I feel relieved, as if I'd finished what was long overdue."

On that note of respite, she faded and contracted, became a firefly again, and zigzagged out the window, toward the ilex trees and the summer outdoors. It was hot. He could not but ponder that, even in the best of times, any given half of humanity will always complain about the other half. But he couldn't think much beyond that. Perhaps he was drugged by the mint and rosemary and verbena, which floated to the nostrils and numbed one's wits, that summertime. In his memoirs, Harold Acton wrote: "In the warm water of the central fountain frogs forgot to leap into hiding under the flat lily leaves and stared upwards as if hypnotized while thirsty dragonflies flashed past for a quick sip and bloated goldfish mouthed at insects drunk with honeysuckle."

In Which Candido Meets the Ghost of Harold Acton, CBE

Purgatory

The vapors

Candido wanted advice for the restoration of the villa from someone who knew villas well and was so disposed. Ideally, it should be a great aesthete. Harold Acton was the perfect candidate, but he was dead! Or was he?

In his villa, Candido kept coming back to the same book, every time he took a visitor, not the obvious dork, but someone who showed signs of literate curiosity and a bent for taste, through the various rooms on the ground floor, and wished to make the point that the value of the library in the villa was not in the discarnate texts, but in its *livres-objets*. They spoke of a family, a period, a social network, and a habit of reading. Like everything in the house, it was the aura—called by Italians *l'atmosfera*—and not the discrete contents, which merited the most respect. The books would be cataloged using the latest techniques, and they could be repaired and cleaned, but they would not be moved or removed from their original place. The vast majority of these books could be found in any good library, but not the inscriptions, the notes, the autographs, the manner of their arrangement. The scholars that one day would reside at the villa would be keen not just on what the volumes said but on how they came to be there, on who knew whom, on how they were written, and read, not on the text but on the sub, the inter-, and the meta-text.

His chosen sample was on a shelf behind the desk in the *studiolo*: a first edition, published in London by James R. Osgood, McIlvaine & Co., in 1891. The book had a pleasing size and felt good to the touch. It was bound in the original light-green cloth, and contained four mordant and well-crafted essays, among which were two of Candido's favorites: "The Decay of Lying," and "The Truth of Masks." They are from Oscar Wilde's quill at its biting best. To make his point to the visitor, Candido would open the book on the page that showed the author's autograph inscription to Bernard Berenson, then turn to the next page, with Nicky Mariano's inscription to Acton scribbled on it. She wanted him to have the book after B. B.'s death. In the fifties, Berenson had made provisions for his villa, I Tatti, to pass to Harvard, and this, all seem to agree, inspired the owners of the villa to give it a similar destiny. Thus, they came upon the Institute at Global U, after being snubbed by Oxford.

One fine summer day, Candido performed his little library routine, ushered a curious visitor inside the cabinet, went to the chosen shelf, and produced the book. This time, however, he noticed that two long strips of paper were inserted between the pages. The one at the front showed a number and a few words (*number 1445 noncirculating*) penciled by the librarian—a Sardinian library scholar and a gentleman—destined, no doubt, for a future database. The second slip, inserted at the back of the book, was folded in two and had Candido's name on it. He took it with a gesture of surprise and put it, unopened, in his pocket before displaying, as usual, the book, showing the visitor the autograph inscriptions and returning the tome to its niche on the shelf.

In the peace of his own rooms, Candido opened the yellow billet. It was not clear to him whether he was awake, or already half asleep. The handwriting was as unmistakable as it was improbable— the baron's own. The text was enigmatic:

> Amidst all the hustle and the bustle, the
> contractors, the visitors, the students, and your

implacable administrators, there are ghosts. I cannot come to you, but you may visit me. We must talk. If in agreement, leave your word on the reverse of this note, and put it back on the same page. In hope, A.

Shouldn't it be H., not A.? was Candido's first thought. But then, there could be a reason. The two letters were valid, the *A* being more properly Oxonian, and they had similar shapes. Like everything with him, it was a matter of tilt. And the signature was, he was sure, from the same pen. Candido answered promptly: "I will visit. Please leave instructions on how, where, and when." He replaced the note in the book and the tome on the shelf. He only had to wait.

When the response came, a week had passed. Candido was not sure if in real or in abridged dreamtime. A new note appeared in the same place. "Please come to this address on August 14, at 10:00 a.m." Simple but strict instructions followed: a street, a number, what names to invoke, and what to expect—the latter in a funny, circuitous way. "If you wish an initiation, consult my best enemy and friend, the Fawn. *Brideshead Revisited*, book two, chapter two." This time, he signed *H.* He was playing games, of the literary sort. The Fawn was Evelyn Waugh, and his book, quite visible on one of the shelves, was next to Graham Greene.

The baths

It was not without some trepidation that Candido asked the taxi driver to leave him at the assigned corner, near the *Piazza del Limbo*. Once there, he followed the Borgo SS. Apostoli, until he reached number sixteen. It was a narrow medieval street in the tourist heart of the city yet miraculously away from the crowds. To his right stood the little piazza and the small portico with a slightly damaged inscription on a slab of *pietra serena*. It read *Bagni nelle Antiche Terme*. The portal led to a small courtyard, which showed one boutique. Next to the store, he found a door with a discreet plate in bronze: *Palestra Ogni Speranza. Members Only.* That was the exact place. He rang the bell, waited a while and, once buzzed, pushed the door. The counter, the crapulous-looking, natty man behind it, the key boxes, the cash register, and the roster book gave the place the semblance of a paddle court, or a cheap hotel. Candido's ghostly friend had chosen a *louche* little establishment, a seedy pansy club for us to meet.

"*Bon giorno. Il suo numero di tessera, prego.*" ("Good day. Your member number, please.") The man pointed with his finger to the book. Candido wrote down 666, as was agreed.

"Ho *un appuntamento con Antonio.*" (I have an appointment with Antonio.) That's what Candido had been asked to say.

"*Il suo nome?*" ("Your name?")

"*Cristoforo.*" (His Catholic confirmation name, used as a code.)

The man called someone inside: "*Virgilio! C'è un signore qui. Si chiama Cristoforo e cerca il Tony.*" (Virgil! There is a gentleman here. His name is Christopher and is looking for Tony.)

"*Un attimo.*" (Just a second.) He went inside. A few minutes passed before somebody else came. The second man was tall, in his twenties, wore a T-shirt and shorts but no shoes, looked Brazilian, and sported a melancholy smile. He carried a large white towel and a little key on a string.

"*Lieto. Venga con me. Gli faccio strada.*" (Pleased to meet you. Come with me. I'll show you the way.) They walked down a corridor toward the lockers. He asked Candido to change and follow him to the steam baths. There was nothing to fear, he said. The establishment was empty because of the early hour, and because of the month (it was *Ferragosto* exactly, just before *la notte di San Lorenzo*, when the sky is full with shooting stars). But Antonio would come, he assured Candido. He smiled, a bit sadly, and waited outside while Candido left his clothes in a locker and, wrapped in a towel gown, emerged in the guise of a Roman senator, almost. The weary usher led him next past a bar, a workout space, a TV lounge, and finally left him at the door of what turned out to be a vast, ill-lit, moldy, fog-ridden, and cavernous room.

Candido pushed the glass door and walked slowly into the vapors. It was dark and silent. He shuddered and shivered, despite the heat. The light was dim, and the hissing of a steam pipe could be heard from time to time. Against what could have been a back wall, he thought he saw some shapes or shadows. He sat down on a tiled bench. The minutes passed, and then he heard a voice.

"*Professore*, we meet *at last!*" There was a pause. "Please call me Harold. I hate Tony, which is a writer's caricature of me, and which I must bear as part of the necessary atonement. May I call you Bigordi?"

"Of course. Or Candido, if you prefer. I am very pleased that we finally meet, although I would have preferred a drink at your old corner table in Harry's Bar."

"I too should favor a few chilled *Bellini* and truffled *tramezzini* on a pink tablecloth. It is impossible, I assure you. Here instead we can talk and will be most inconspicuous. Not quite your milieu, my dear, but mine. At present, this is my home."

"Well," Candido said, affecting an ease he was far from feeling in that den, "what have you been up to all these years?"

"My dear, it is what *you* have been up to that we are here to talk about. I'm a faithful old spirit, and I've kept my eye on you. I visited your villa—without being seen of course—several times since your arrival, and found what you have done in general quite strong and correct. The enormous works on the roof, your guidelines for the rooms, your love of the gardens, your very notion that the future of the estate should follow, in spirit and aim, what the Rockefellers, whom I once knew, have done at Pocantico Hills, which are all splendid. I would not have had the courage. But be careful, my dear; that is *not* what your superiors would prefer."

"That is why I hurry to make decisions that will be very hard to reverse. In the meantime, I endeavor to persuade them to do the right thing."

"I wouldn't have such faith in adult education. They are spoiled by money and intoxicated by what they mistake as power. They think, my dear, they know best. They'd *love* to add a few teeth to Mona Lisa's smile, or adjust the Tower of Pisa to fix that lean. You will be able to postpone, not avoid, a collision. May that take long, I pray."

"Perhaps. But your support is of great help."

"It is *you*, my dear, who will help *me*."

"You must explain. You see, we must speak about you."

"Alas, you're quite right. I will explain. I am here because during my life, I was Janus-faced. One part of me was English, with a keen zest to be well bred. The other part abhorred both English snobbery and English morals, and would have preferred to be entirely a degenerate old d-d-dago." (His voice hesitated for a moment, and I thought I heard a stutter.) "Until I solve my dilemma, I will not leave these rooms: the gym, the bar, the baths, the vulgar music, the sniggering youths."

"So, how *do* you spend your days? What do you do?"

"To grope, to fail, and then to cope, is the purgatory exercise I am condemned to repeat day after day, in this twilight zone of steam. The saucy boys come and go, while I stay, undressed yet unaddressed. Such luscious fruits out of my reach! I was familiar, of course, with the seventh story in Dante's abode of penance, where the lustful are roasted till the lust is burned out of them. I was not prepared, however, to be cooked *au bain Marie*! In this slow cauldron, I am consumed by wishes that I cannot fulfill. I am a horny shadow, not substantial. I am with and inside each of the lads here and I am nowhere too; everything they do, I once did and now redo, but it's nothing too. All I feel is an immense fatigue, accompanied by thought. In life, I was restrained, elegant, and quite a snob. Anger, avarice, were not my sins. I never ate in excess, though I did relish many a good drink. My gluttony was of a different kind: an uncontrollable and ceaseless search after young quivering flesh. That was the vice, but not the sin. The passion I followed *jusqu'à la folie* might have been the path to greater things, as only art can embody and sublimate. It was the way of many great Florentines. But when the artist fails, what remains is the aesthete: a gesture, an empty pose, the fatuous mien, and a prurient prick. I now see the thin veil that separates a health spa from a sordid bath, a spurt of creative love from a shabby fucking episode. No, no, the vice is not important. What counts is *the waste—le temps perdu*—the nightmare of my soul, the return of that dark moment when Ezra Pound, whom I adored, dismissed me as a mediocre bore at my own lunch table."

"You seem embarked on a belated program to make up for time lost."

"Desperately *à la recherche du temps perdu*! You can quicken my quest."

"How so?"

"Persevere in your job, and watch your back—*guarda le spalle*. The villa is in peril, as are my own and many others. I know it, and you know it too. It can be swamped, transmogrified, defiled. If it loses its karma, I and my ghostly friends will lose our souls. In my own case, by giving it in trust, I honored my ancestors and set it on a course to a high destiny. I meant to buy back my waywardness in a true act of love. If my wishes are betrayed, like those of many dearly departed, I shall have little hope of speedy mercy. If our legacy in the villas of Tuscany becomes a tasteless monument to waste, we will surely fall from the precarious point on which we are perched to the very depths of hell."

"I understand what may go wrong, and I solemnly promise to do what I can. It may, however, prove quite tough, beyond my strength."

"I know, but you are strong—*molto deciso*—when a good cause is at stake. You can convince, compromise up to a point, even seduce, and you can also grandstand. The opportunity is unique: Italy will like you; America should support. But you will find allies and enemies in unexpected places. We are both Catholic, so you know that good judgment—a pale copy of the divine—appears to the loveless as wrath and to the loving as mercy. You will see that in the end, *Omnia vincit Amor*, as the young man who ushered you to me likes to say, although I am not sure what he has in mind. This, and no other, is the reason why we are having this exchange. Selfless love is a two-way street. Tit for tat: us in the afterlife can encourage you by our awareness of your love. I can, if you indulge me with your patience, give you a few secrets and some tips."

"A talisman?"

"Too strong a word, my dear. Let's just say a hint or two."

"Give me the first."

"In my life, I published several collections of short stories. Not well received, but I did my best. In one of them I call my villa *La Trappola* (*The Trap*)—a good name, don't you think? In another one, I wrote about a man not unlike myself, who lived in a vast villa, enjoyed its beauty and its peace. He abhorred to be disturbed, especially by functionaries. One day, he found, by accident, the fragments of a fresco which had been whitewashed. He then made a terrible mistake: he reported the find to the *Belle Arti*! The functionaries came. They took measurements and pictures, discussed among themselves, and treated the poor owner as if *they* owned the place. They used their power to order the entire fresco exposed at the silenced man's expense. The house was invaded by experts of all kinds, ordering workers around, placing scaffolds here and there until the job was done. The exposed fresco was a fiasco—an ugly exercise by a long-dead nincompoop. The functionaries got promotions. The owner's pockets, his peace, his very life, were ruined in return."

"I appreciate the little nightmare, but fail to see the point, unless—"

"Exactly. Unless it's based on truth. I once *did* find the fragments of a fresco in a corridor on the second floor of my villa. And, I assure you, it's not the only one. My parents' bedroom has more. And I bet you have the same in your own villa. You see, my dear, what today are rooms were open galleries some centuries ago. And they were decorated in a colorful and profuse way by young artists favored in those days. At the old house in Montughi, three might have worked on those walls: Boticelli, Lippi, and your own *antenato, caro Corradi*."

"And who was that?"

"Domenico, of course. Il Ghirlandaio. He worked for Sassetti, as you well know."

"Was he the artist in your villa?"

"I think so. And in yours too. The fragments I discovered show magnificent *puttini*, in full flight, laced by ribbons. The incision is firm, but the result is gentle and gay. Such trace and grace might only be the work of Domenico—unless they are a divertimento by his friend Filippino."

"And you hid it all."

"Of course. I was terrified of an invasion. I covered my *puttini* promptly with a console and kept the secret, but it tortured me. So I let it out, and all my fears, in fiction. I changed the details, and gave the literary fresco a shabby provenance. The real one is different. It is an unexploded bomb."

"And I thought I would only find skeletons in those walls."

"No, mostly *puttini*. But if one day, my dear, you find too many American *puttane* prancing by those walls, if the villa is used for weddings and bar mitzvahs, just detonate the bomb. Better in that case to have the *Belle arti* stop them on their tracks."

"I promise you I will do, if the situation calls for it. If the existence of important frescoes is revealed, the official and the public interest would stop any devious plan, as you say, on its tracks. But in the end, only a scientific approach can determine what the incisions on the wall are, and even who placed them there. If they turn out to be second-rate *sgrafitto*, nothing much will follow."

"I know. My dear, there are already devious plans afoot. In my present state, I can visit all counsels, no matter how secret; my ears pierce all walls."

"I will check with an *ingegnere* friend of mine, who has x-ray machines that can also pierce the walls without damaging anything."

"There is the plan to install air-conditioning."

"They call it climate control."

"It is extremely expensive when properly done. The aim is to maintain a constant temperature and humidity in all the rooms, to preserve the art from the wild swings of the seasons."

"It was done for centuries *a la nostrale*, by opening and closing shutters, letting the air, but not the light, in during summers, and firing gentle heating when it was cold."

"But now there is an elaborate security system in place, which forbids such movements. There are no more servants who know what to do."

"Bah. Expensive convolutions to arrive at the same point. There's America at her worst: people buy treadmills because they forget how to walk."

"How true, but it's the universal trend, in Europe too. I've visited the Jacquemard-André house museum, the Rothschild villa on Cap Ferrat, I Tatti, as well as the Newport Mansions, the Rockefeller's Kykuit, and Dumbarton Oaks. They do the same thing. For many, good AC, central heating, and American-style comfort count for more than memories."

"You must prevent 'progress' from messing this one up."

"What worries me most is the use."

"It was left for a steady stream of few and selected scholars to find peace and inspiration, to converse over tea, to write their books. A document I wrote in the nineteen fifties made it clear when I wrote plans for my villa after my death. I remember it by heart:

> The villa is not to be a college or a graduate school but a research center for advanced and qualified scholars. It should not have a formal curriculum. Their foremost need is to follow their researches and to write in a atmosphere free from other academic responsibilities.

"It sounds secretive. How would you recruit such tenants?"

"I am sure the villa would amply fulfill this yearning. I did not want its celebrity brashly flaunted. It would not be in any way indebted to publicity; it would rest upon words transmitted with love by word of mouth among the truly cognoscenti. It would rely on a tacit agreement."

"A literary Freemasonry?"

"Precisely."

"Do you think that is what the powers that be really want for my villa?"

"I doubt it very much. For them, useless knowledge is not sublime, just useless. They want an undergraduate college in the site, with plenty of PR. As for the palace, they will end up building little apartments in the attic, and use the lordly rooms for parties and for guests to roam."

"But how will they be assigned?"

"To favorite cronies, to families with brats, to donors and friends, to many a pompous ass. Remember, my dear: *they have no class.*"

"Your taste is an endangered species."

"*Rara avis*, yes. To conserve it, we must restore its habitat. That's why my property was left in private hands. It could have gone to the city, but it seems to me that government-run treasures are poorly protected or even poached, dispersed, with the connivance of corrupt politicians, and in the end exist only on paper. That is one reason villas are sometimes left to a private institution which would not be motivated primarily by money, with an endowment fund to pay for the estate's protection in perpetuity. I always dreamt of an institute of higher learning, with trustees who care spiritually, almost religiously, about such site."

"Noble sentiments, sir Harold. And ones that seem to motivate many custodians of beauty around the world. But you must know that universities are often torn between those values and the pursuit of a steady stream of income in the form of student revenues and other more dubious schemes to take money from whatever and whomever."

"If that prevails, there will be little hope for the precious habitat."

"So how am I to protect the villa from time-shares and unsavory crowds?"

"Count on Florence, on its immense resources of subtlety and intrigue. Its proven incapacity to gets things done is more than matched by its superlative ability to stop whatever might be done. Old evil against crassness: it's an uneven fight."

"Asymmetrical warfare?"

"Perhaps. If you succeed, you will become truly an honorary citizen. Florence will never be on your passport, but always in your mind—and you carry a bit of it in your genes. Left, right, Catholic, heathen, or Jew: it does not matter. Florence is not a place or a frontier, it is a grammar that only a few can master."

"Talk to the *soprintendente*. Open to him you heart. You can be friends. He's a good man; he comes from Rome. The opportunity will soon arise. You have friends in common. There will be many parties, dinners by candlelight, and strolls around the park. He will ask, in the end, for you to form a committee on good taste, composed of proper individuals, to help, to advise, to guide in the delicate restorations on which you are to embark. They will know how to act, or rather, to stop unwelcome action."

"Will they confront the barbarians?"

"No. But they'll watch, and they'll be arch. Remember, my dear, Cavafy's poem: the barbarians are, after all, some sort of solution."

"Florentine lesson one."

"And my tip number two. *Evviva Niccolò!*"

"I am beginning to understand. Good old Machiavelli. There is so much I must know."

"So many years, so many intrigues. We would spend a lifetime in these baths pondering them all: my loves, my travels, my friends, the dirty linen of the Florentines, the crooks that have surrounded me, especially the triumvirate of lawyer, architect, and my own secretary. In my prime, I was a famous gossip. When I declined, I was duped, so there's some gossip left for the afterlife."

"Anything I should be aware of, some immediate danger?"

"*Cave avocatum. Un uomo molto discusso.* (Beware the lawyer. He is a piece of work.) The university Italian lawyer will try to befriend you. As your friend, the marchesa says, Ha *l'anima nera* (dark soul), that one. A regular little gold digger. He took from his own mentor, a dear friend of mine, more than the practice, after the gentleman had to run away from the racial laws of Mussolini. And from me, he has gotten a lot! His clutches are on everything: property, power, connections, felonies, and cover-ups, even a drug lord friend whom he is protecting from extradition in Brazil. Like a vampire bat, he takes flight when dusk is falling. When it comes to the wills of old men, first he insinuates an idea, then he guides their hands, and finally he makes them sign what they no longer understand—a shaky scribble on a well-prepared piece of paper, with paid witnesses, before the last breath. *Scava, scava, il cacciatore di dote.*"

"I'm short of breath myself. The heat, the steam, and all these stories."

"I had forgotten. How time has passed! It's time for you, my dear, to rejoin the world outside. Go back to the sunlight. I will keep watching over you. You will get further hints from me."

"I'll heed all good advice."

"You will find an old manuscript in one of the drawers of my villa. You can procure it from the librarian. It is the plot of a murder mystery which I never managed to publish, but you can pass it along to a common friend who might. The murder which almost takes place—of someone not unlike yourself—is meant to hide a different, near-perfect crime, which your *doppelganger,* your double, was about to spoil."

"Let's not take our leave on such a macabre note."

"Do not worry. *You*, my dear, are bulletproof, and shall in the end get the desserts of the just. If worse comes to worst, remember your namesake Candide: he suffered a lot, but in the end he survived it all. As for me, if your mission fails and also my own villa is debased, before I go to hell, I'll do everything to finish it completely, turn it into a brothel, or a hospice, or make it burst in flames. I'd rather enter hell with a blast!" Even when he contemplated defeat, sir Harold could not avoid delusions of grandeur.

A youth opened the door to the steam room at that moment.

"Don't be a tease, Tony. I know you are there. Come out and buy me a drink." Candido remembered another appointment and left the baron to deal with him.

"Have a good day," he said.

As Candido left, he mumbled, he did not know why, half to the ghost, half to himself, "I shall do my best. And to you, good night, poor baron. May not these pathetic youths but flights of angels come to the rescue and sing you to your rest."

Candido retraced his steps, passed the bar and the gym, into the changing room. Half a dozen boys were drinking and playing with a slot machine. He was soon outdoors, back on the straight street. It was midafternoon, and Florence was muggy and empty.

In Which a Technical Procedure Leads to a Discovery That Seems Momentous but Falls Flat in Disappointment

Egregio Ingegnere Dottore
Gianfranco Aldobrandini
Via dei Santi, 22
1025 Firenze

Dear Ingegnere:

This is a message to firm up the details of your forthcoming lecture at our campus in Florence, planned for April 13, at 6:00 p.m., on the general subject of "A Renaissance Villa: Aspects of Restoration." I would like to propose that your talk be announced as "Resurgence of Things Past: The Use of Modern Technology in the Service of Art and Architectural History." We would love it if you could not only present some of your findings from thermography at our villa but also some of the remarkable work you have done with paintings in the Palazzo Vecchio, as you were kind enough to show my wife and me in your studio.

We are ready to send invitations and a program to the printer, so I would like to have your okay and confirmation at your earliest convenience.

With kind regards,
Candido Bigordi
Executive Director

Candido had read about Ingegnere Aldobrandini in an article published in the Florentine press, in which he was portrayed as a modern iconoclast who regularly challenged the theories of art by historians about famous paintings. Against classic interpretations based on aesthetic hunches and scholarly inferences, the *ingegenere* used the blunt method of science: he owned a series of, to shocked traditionalists, devilish machines that actually "saw" whatever was hidden on a canvas, or a wall. Oftentimes, his verdict was hard, if not impossible, to appeal; it came down on many a distinguished neck like a polished axe of reason. Many reputations risked irreparable damage from the revelations of this quiet, well-poised man, prone to present his case with the unflappable authority of a neurosurgeon, or the cold matter-of-factness of an executioner. He threatened to put some pundits out of business, and the closed community of art scholars, showing a rare case of corporate solidarity, shunned him like a leper. They tried, whenever possible, to bad-mouth his methods and credentials. The plight of the *ingegnere,* his status as a learned underdog, immediately endeared him to Candido. Mutual sympathy grew into a complicitous friendship when one day, at a cocktail party, the two realized they shared a common past in gentle La Jolla, California, as disciples of the same German philosopher who held old-fashioned, romantic views about aesthetics with obstinate consistency—*mit tierischen Ernst.* They shared a disappointment with their mentor's late little tome, *The Aesthetic Dimension.*

As the villa needed some serious structural repair, it was not difficult for Bigordi to hire Aldobrandini to use the latest techniques of thermal analysis and draw a virtual sketch of the palace in its various incarnations through the ages. Modern thermal cameras, properly trained on the walls in the sweet evening twilight of Tuscany, when sunset is followed by a temperature inversion, and buildings begin to cool off—that is, to release the great heat accumulated during daylight, reveal, thanks to the different cooling rates of various materials, ancient structures, former windows, presently blocked and plastered over, bygone arches, ceilings that were lower than the current ones. The heat emanating from the walls projects a shadow, and in that shadow, it is possible to see the ghost of a room as it was centuries ago. And all this is perfectly traced and recorded, in a stunning gamut of colors, by a smart program on a computer screen, and is saved in the computer memory. Aldobrandini's machine did its magic, and the imagination took flight, like the owl of Minerva, when dusk was falling. The procedure produced real-time snapshots of forgotten moments of the palace—a scientific gallery of ghostly shapes.

The *ingegnere* had other tricks in his magic bag: x-ray cameras, UV cameras, infrared devices that he could, in the wee hours, train on paintings and on painted walls. As their friendship grew, and Aldobrandini's official job progressed, Candido convinced Aldobrandini to join him in a little conspiracy, a peep show escapade to the hidden frescoes that obsessed sir Harold so. To provide a suitable cover to that nocturnal extracurricular work, they chose not deception, but the truth, and fully exposed the method—though not their plot—to the public. For the record, they feigned all the proprieties of men who didn't know each other, let alone hatch secret schemes.

Dear Dottore,

Thank you very much for your invitation. I would love to give an overall presentation about the most interesting findings derived from applied technologies to art and architectural history.

Unfortunately, I do have a problem about the scheduled date (April 27) of the lecture. From the 24th to the 29th of April, I have been invited to Cleveland to attend the annual American Museums Association Convention.

Any other time will be fine. I sincerely hope this inconvenience will not mess up this wonderful possibility you are offering me.

With cordial regards,
Gianfranco Aldobrandini

In the end, the lecture did take place and was a resounding success. Among the attending Florentines, it made the not altogether honest impression that Global U really cared about conservation and was eager to discover whatever hidden treasures the villa contained. It kindled a keen interest among key people in the new techniques of research in the history of art. Last, but not least, it made public the quest that Gianfranco and Candido intended to pursue in secrecy, under cover of darkness. As with the famous purloined letter, full sight was the best hiding place—except that in this case, they pursued their quest under cover of darkness.

It was midnight in the villa. The alarms had been turned off at Candido's request.

"What we see now is not the final fresco, but the remnants of older work under the paint." Gianfranco had pointed the infrared camera to the upper right-hand corner of the wall. The two of them were staring at an adjacent computer monitor. It revealed what the machine saw under the whitewash—a miracle of infrared reflectography. It was actually past midnight, the usual hour when they met and chatted, over coffee, in total darkness, except for the glow of the liquid crystal screen. Most of the equipment Gianfranco used—x-rays, infrared cameras, sonograms, and ultraviolet light—he had adapted from the medical field. Like vampires, his devices abhorred daylight. He thought of himself as a doctor whose patients were works of art.

"I think it's an older fresco, degraded and painted over by the same artist or by someone else."

"Gianfranco, the faded work is, I think, Baldovinetti's, or someone like him. You see, he mixed his colors with egg yolk and boiled varnish, believing that the frescoes would be preserved from damp. He made wonderful concoctions. The effect was intense, but the results were disastrous. The paint dropped from the wall after a year or so! His disciples returned to the traditional methods of fresco and tempera. The results were not as rich or deep in color, but they lasted, as you can see from the later layers."

"Amazing. How do you know that?"

"It's only a hunch. I read about it. Vasari mentions a chapel in Santa Trìnita, later destroyed in the eighteenth century, as an instance of Baldovinetti's failed technique."

"If that was the case here as well, then who did the fresco on top of it?"

"Oh…one of his pupils, I suppose, with better chemical sense than the master but not as good a hand. After all, what was good enough for Masaccio was good enough for him. Please, do me a favor, turn the camera more to your left."

Gianfranco moved the camera down and to the left. The monitor showed an array of figures. These were remarkably well preserved.

"You must be right. Look at this! It is the work of a different hand. There is a direct simplicity of handling, and the figures seem to be in great shape."'

"I'm glad the avoidance of dangerous methods has paid off, after five hundred years."

The first object to appear was an open balustrade, letting in a view of a mountainous landscape descending to the sea. The image on the monitor was not very clear. But soon a figure appeared, very neat, in front of the balustrade, a simple and happy composition of low-toned flesh. Then a second figure, and a third.

"They are saints."

"Maybe they are angels; see the wings?"

"You are right. Angels and saints, in those days, were pretexts for portraits. These seem to be boys, fifteen the younger one, seventeen or eighteen the other two, I would say. Probably local kids from the neighborhood or the workshop. That one looks like Ghirlandaio's rendering of Amerigo Vespucci in Ognissanti. But it is not of the same quality. A version perhaps by an apprentice of the same Corradi *bottegha.*"

They were looking at a young man in a green under-dress, with his right hand outstretched, wings caught in early deployment, and the lower part of his body enveloped in a toga-like mantle. The Florentine civil dress had been made to assume a classical shape. The head seemed to have been cut out and replaced on fresh intonaco. In general, the religious element in the picture was overburdened by a sense of everydayness, and sex.

"The next angel is special. Do you think this one is also a portrait?"

"Not a portrait at all. He is too idealized. This is not meant to be just a pretty painted face but a soul. In any case that seems the intent. The quality is not great. I think all these characters are exercises by common pupils."

We could not take our eyes from that face which grew larger as we zoomed the camera, like a sun which it was somehow possible to stare at and which was coming nearer and nearer, letting itself be seen at close quarters, dazzling us with its blaze of reddish gold. But the closer we got, the coarser the face seemed.

"Only Botticelli or Lippi ever painted faces as full of dreamy mystery as this young unknown Florentine tried to imitate. But clearly, he failed. This one is almost grotesque."

"Then this could not be a very important find."

"Not really. Of some interest perhaps, but nothing to brag about."

"I can still feel some passion in these frescoes. But passion is never enough. They are second class, maybe third."

Aldobrandini did not mince words. He was used to great masters, and these faded frescoes disappointed him.

"What is missing here is the old Florentine impulse."

"It's in the blood, I guess. I understand the old urge. A beautiful face drawn by a maestro suddenly glides into the field of vision of a young boy named Domenico, Leonardo, or Michelangelo. The boy copies the face, then copies the face again: a sequence of faces—an angel, two, a woman and child, a saint. The copying doesn't stop. It floods the city, it crowds the world. I have uncovered other angels that want to fly, to reveal themselves, to multiply in legions, to shine forth and through, but not these hidden frescoes. The three ones here have been captives of a hideous wall for very long, but I think they are best left there."

"Harold Acton thought they were masterpieces, or early works by true maestros, and was afraid their discovery would lead to endless bureaucratic meddling."

"I have not seen the ones he claimed are in his place, but I bet they are of the same ilk. He did well in hiding them, not because they are great, but because they are not worth the trouble."

"So their discovery would not lead to publicity and a scandal, but produce a mere shrug."

"The authorities could still close the place down."

"It reminds me of a sign I saw in a shop once in a forsaken dusty town in Arkansas: 'We buy junk and sell antiques.'"

"Exactly. They seem authentic, but so what? Like so many things in this palace, the pretense is great, but the reality is mediocre."

"Poor baron, he counted on works like these in extremis to save his villa, similar to this one in the neighborhood, from modernization."

"Actually, in disguising what he thought was true in his published story, he was unwittingly disclosing the truth. There was nothing there, and there is nothing here to write home about."

"In Florence, nothing is what it seems. The truth dances with the lie in dizzying pirouettes."

"The efforts then and the efforts now share one thing in common: the poverty of imagination."

We moved the credenza back against the wall, and covered the faded frescoes just as they were before.

Aldobrandini let with a lapidary statement:

"This villa is not a chef d'oeuvre like I Collazzi; it is more a Villa Fiasco."

The Detective

In Which Candido Discovers a Murder Plot

The draft

Things were not going well for *il direttore* Bigordi at the villa. Every proposal of substance he submitted was first delayed, then denied. His American bosses were only interested in the "study abroad" part of the program. It promised to be lucrative, increase enrollments, and bring money and kids in spades. But what about high-level studies and policy discussions, transatlantic relations, the future of the European Union, and the best way for America to benefit from it, and for it to be protected by America and the United Kingdom (America's best friend inside the EU) from the encroachments of a rising Russia and an expanding China? There was no great interest in such things. A serious collaboration with the European University Institute next door? Better leave it alone, perhaps one day.

And so it went, week after week, month after month, while there was ever-mounting pressure to provide beds and classrooms, temporary instructors, panini and cafeterias for a growing contingent of demanding undergraduates—brats who thought that because their parents paid, they deserved good grades. An improvised hospitality industry was born. Like a faulty passenger jet, in the famous expression of someone in the airline business, it sometimes looked like a contraption designed by clowns and supervised by apes. The program at least would not produce deadly crashes.

To appease his growing despair, Candido visited Harold's villa and under a pretext, searched for Harold's draft. At least it could provide some distraction and a palliative for his wounded soul. Somehow, he felt an affinity with Harold's ghost—a growing *simpatia*—as if they were both in the same limbo, victims of a seemingly benign, but in reality insidious, betrayal. They shared the same suspicions. In some cases, they were both right, and in other cases equally wrong.

The text promised by Harold's ghost in the bathhouse appeared in a drawer in his villa, mixed with old invoices, a dinner menu, and the corrected proofs of *Puttini e Puttane*, a racy and posthumous book with a funny title penned by his friend don Nanni Guiso. Candido made a photocopy of Harold's draft, graciously lent by a friendly secretary, and left the original in its proper spot. It was never found again. Harold's lawyer or his former secretary probably destroyed it, for it struck too close to home. Candido read and reread the copy at his leisure, a deed for which he thanked myself, for when he lost the text with other papers one distracted afternoon on the train to Bologna, he had almost memorized it. He could transcribe what he could recollect, in its untidy entirety, and it was quite a lot.

"The exercise in narrative prose that follows was written in 1989, and should be modified, out of kindness, after my death. It stems, I believe, from my readings, in a translation by Norman Thomas di Giovanni, of don Jorge Luis Borges, and from some movies I saw in Paris, in my visits to that film-addicted town over several decades. It exploits certain tricks, like shifts in continuity, and the condensation of a man's whole life into two or three scenes. The story does not seek to be psychological but logical and then seemingly illogical, to present the reader with some heinous deeds. It might easily devolve upon a common murder mystery. *E rimasta soltanto una bozza.* (It is just a draft.) A good crime writer like Magda Nabb might take it one day and polish it appropriately. The story starts with a gigolo—a young boy of confidence and a confident man that will take over the life of an elderly gentleman.

Daz Gabor is what I shall call him, for this was the name he was known by, around 1960, in the streets and *vicoli* of Rome. The registry of births in Hamburg lists him as Johannes Friedrich Schult, and enters the name under the date April 1, 1940, in the middle of the war. It is known that he was a photographer's son, that his father was presumed dead, *Totgesagt*, according to the *Wehrmacht*, at the Russian front, that his mother disappeared one day too, that his childhood suffered the drabness and squalor of bombed-out slums, and that he felt the call of the sea. Running away to sea is, strictly speaking, more an English than a German thing to do, but then Hamburg is a great port. Geography fosters the impulse, and so does the Bible: "They that go down to the sea in ships, that do business in great waters; These see the works of the Lord, and his wonders in the deep" (Psalm 107).

Schult ran away from his familiar, hunger-stricken, burned-down streets by the wharfs, and from the humanitarian whores that supported him, went down to the sea in a ship, gazed first at the Big Dipper, then at the Southern Cross, and jumped ship in the port of Buenos Aires. As an individual, he was quiet and dull. He could easily have starved, but his good looks, his fixed smile, and his accommodating disposition brought him under the wing of a Hungarian family of refugees, called Gabor, whose name he came to adopt.

In Buenos Aires, he liked to keep the company of a blind writer, who had the gracious habit of paying his tab at a small café in a corner of Buenos Aires. It actually consisted of five corners, Las Cinco Esquinas. From that gentle bard, he learned the lyrics of many tangos, and of that fast-paced cousin of the tango, the milonga. Some of those words kept, for many years, sounding in his mind:

> *Parado en las Cinco Esquinas*
> *Con toda mi contingencia,*
> *Por ver si te rompo el culo*
> *Ando haciendo diligencia.*

> I'm standing in these five corners
> With everything I got
> Following all due procedure
> To see if I can bust your ass.

His poet friend was funny. "What strikes me most about these milonga verses is the contrast between the bureaucratic formality and the violent upshot," he said in a soft, melodious voice.

Of this Argentine episode, no other traces are left, but his gratitude never flagged, since, in 1962, he reappears in Italy, in a villa near Rome, still using the adopted name Daz Gabor. There he befriended another older gentleman, who took a shining to him, and who knew, or suspected, but did not mind at all, Gabor's meandering *parcours*.

Traveling in Europe, back from his seafaring avatars, Daz finds himself alone and without money, so he looks around and soon discovers that the world—especially the international playgrounds of Italy and the South of France—is well blessed with the rich and the elderly and the lonely, many of whom are only too pleased to receive the attentions of the young and the beautiful, be they boys or girls. It pleases their vanity, and they can afford the price. There are many to choose from, and when our hero sets his mind to it, he can be alluring. He can take his pick. In those playgrounds, many spend their youth chasing money; others their money chasing youth. As for our youth's amorous preferences, well, he cavorts with members of each sex. Perhaps he has left a boyhood sweetheart in Hamburg or Buenos Aires, to expand his horizons, and to whet his tastes.

In Fez, or was it Alexandria, our young pilgrim meets a merchant, Annuar El Zizi, who teaches him an Arab story about the practices of males in those parts. It stays in his mind. "We do it," he is told, "with women for procreation, with boys for love, and with sheep for satisfaction." On procreation, Daz is not terribly keen. He abhors marriage. He is not attracted to women, although he can seduce them. As for satisfaction, nothing rivals the taste of good food in nice surroundings, and large quantities of wine. Sheep are best consumed when properly cooked in the manner of the Mont St. Michel, as *pré salé*. On love, he is willing to follow the gentleman's advances and advice, with some modifications, of the venal kind. Since pedagogy and ambition are important considerations, it is better to be a protege to a distinguished daddy, he reckons, like the Argentine Gabriel Yturri with the Count de Montesquiou-Fezenac, than find similar twinks in the many haunts where he may score. It is not only Arabian but classic Greek as well. *If I am to be a hustler*, he mused, *I'd rather do it in style.*

One day, Daz arrives in the old villa, *La Sparita*, tucked away at the foot of the Lepini Mountains, south of Rome, and is presented to the master as a poor artist by a young writer of their common acquaintance, and bent. His clothes are more or less in tatters, but his saucy looks (under the clothes) and *savoir faire* do not escape the thirsty glance of the older gentleman, Prince Lauro Gibbons Cerretani, who is leading the life of a recluse, alone with Mom, an Englishwoman who, between the wars, and especially during the reign of fascism in Italy, made the estate a literary refuge for writers. Despondent in old age, the lady has become difficult and drinks too much. She is always with a glass in her hand, robed in Chinese gowns. Now she has taken to share the martinis and the silks with her son. The two make an aloof, unhappy pair.

Our hero manages to stay over. Daz has a long, rambling conversation with the prince as they walk the length of the *vialone*, or green avenue, under the great umbrella pines. They cover many subjects in French and English, and share a few off-colored jokes. The boy lets his buns be pinched, and laughs a hearty laugh. The budding romance does not escape the gardeners, busy pruning the yew and boxwood hedges. They have seen other such buds and buns before. *Ah finocchi*, the fennel fields of Italia, the arbors and ardors behind her sinful palace walls! Our young man is invited to spend a few days, and nights, in the old villa, whence he emerges changed: no longer *Pissenkunstler* but handsome gigolo. Mama is charmed, and she doesn't mind.

The relationship lasts thirty years. It has, of course, its many ups and downs. The old gentleman does not want anything "steady"—*quel horreur*! The scope of his interest in men is too ecumenical. (Closets in those days were places one put clothes in, not places whence anyone came out.)

Besides their main affair, did Daz really pimp for the baron? Did the baron need anyone to pimp for him? Perhaps, but it's not clear in retrospect. Daz engaged in late-night escapades, hunting for youths, but these tended to be of a lower class. The baron keeps an impeccable profile of a snob of the belle epoque. He prefers to flirt with young literati and aesthetes. Besides, other more important things occupy his mind. He no longer harbors hopes as a poet, but he keeps writing short stories, and becomes even more passionately a historian. The history of decadence is what attracts him most. He reads voraciously and writes profusely. He peruses archives. He works on his memoirs, which he properly deodorizes. Always respectful of form, he is perhaps too meticulous for his own good, too afraid of the faux pas, or the confession, to write with energy and abandon, but can't help it. He continues and expands the tradition of his household, to lavishly entertain. He becomes prolific and famous. The last thing he wants is to be seen in a "couple" situation, like those pairs of aging *pédales*, as he says, who trot their joint scars and catty squabbles in the sunlight. He has always preferred variety, the ephemeral and surreptitious, to the near-institutional obligation to love someone with whom one is stuck by a long-forgotten episode of passion. How he longs for the grand yet carefree days of princely living, poetry, and love for hire in the specialized establishments of Paris, Beijing or Bangkok! In Italy, he keeps himself distant, lonely, and exquisitely polite.

But with age come weakness and dependency. The prince needs a secretary in whom to trust his correspondence, his papers, his dear galley proofs. Someone worldly enough to organize his schedule, his *emploi du temps*, help him in his travels, be a photographer, drive him around, make odd procurements (even in matters of the flesh), and, last but not least, manage his parents' great gem: the gardens.

The gardeners soon learn to regret the complacent chuckles with which they first greeted "the boy." He is now *il signorino*, telling them imperiously what to plant, or uproot, and where—and always changing his mind. He makes some egregious mistakes. He has *magnoliae grandiflorae* planted where they do not belong. He orders the gardeners to uproot the *boschetto*—planted shrubs—surrounding the Temple of Love. No sooner have they done that, that the conventional temple stands naked and ugly upon a barren hill. Worse, without plants to contain the slide, every time it rains, the erosion rapidly destroys the magnificent open theater—*teatro verde*—on the gentle slopes beneath. The lovely garden theater had been the pride and glory of Lauro's parents. There they offered parties, masquerades, *tableaux vivants*, and bucolic ballets, as was the fashion in the belle epoque and then during the roaring twenties. Many pictures are silent witnesses of those events. A later photograph in the archives shows the prince dancing there, hand in hand, with none other than Margot Fontain. The gardeners oblige but detest our hero under their breath. How many times, after his liquid lunch, he barked at them in German, bringing back memories of a dark past? They had all watched *Casablanca*, and applauded when Colonel Strasser gets shot.

Impertinent as he is, often drunk, given to fits of temper, and malicious, *il signorino* becomes, nevertheless, more indispensable with every year and every month that passes. Many a time, the lord of the domain thinks he's had enough and throws him out, only to succumb later to his protégé's profession of penance and declarations of love. For a long time, the cad is exiled in Venice. His love letters—inevitably accompanied by stories of hardship—are properly answered, and rewarded, if not in kind, at least with generous checks. But Daz always returns. In the end, when the old gentleman can barely move or think too clearly, he moves in, this time with several plans in mind and a new mission: to facilitate the transition of the vast property from *il principe* to his heirs, the rulers of a large university in Chicago cited in the will, in light and preparation of the landlord's impending death, and to keep everybody else—many old friends included—out.

Such is the script for a story, written and enacted many times—in novels, thrillers, films, the theater, all based on a few elements of greed, passion, and missteps, and their many permutations. Of these, the lives of several of my friends, and my own life, were not exempt. In the sunset of our lives, our paramount concern was to leave our treasures and possessions to worthy heirs, lest they got dispersed, and vanished without trace.

There was the matter of the wills. *Il principe* Lauro had written several over the years, with slight modifications each time. The last two were critical, and had to be "steered"—with the deft intervention of lawyers—so as to honor not only the prince's wishes but those of other constituencies as well. One, in Italian, and in the prince's own handwriting, would be executed in Rome. The second one, typed in English, and in a language that betrayed expert help from abroad, would be executed in America. Some beneficiaries of earlier wills were deleted; some new ones were added. Daz got Mom's jewels, a hundred million lire, and the use in perpetuity of a large chunk of *La Simonetta*, one of the houses in the estate—with a lemonary included as his own artist studio, and the surrounding gardens as well. The American school got the land it needed for its campus, as required by its plans. In the Italian will, the Polish Institute of Rome inherited the premises it rented from the Cerretanis (they were the founders and patrons) on the Lungotevere. The same *palazzo* housed an antiquarian shop, which produced some rent. The tenant—one Lorenzo, friend of the entourage and Daz's sometime *amichetto*—got lucky as well: his would be the shop. In due course, and after Lauro's death, the same antiquarian, introduced by Daz, would be entrusted by the lucky recipient of the estate and its collections, the up-and-coming global university in Chicago, drawing an inventory of the artwork in the villa—some three thousand objects, by his counting, which was the institute's fiduciary duty to preserve, as per the will(s). The final figure did not, of course, include the two truckloads of goods, art and antiques that were, the gardeners believed, first stored in the kitchen garden of the villa (*hortus conclusus*), then spirited away to destinies unknown soon after Lauro's death. Since the inventory was drawn after the fact of the alleged transportation, there was no trace. (There are records of a suspect auction in the US in which the villa is named.) The gardeners kept quiet, except, eventually and surprisingly, the youngest one, Alberto, with whom Daz had had a tryst or two, and then snubbed and ignored. Alberto, who discovered he was incurably ill, vowed vengeance, but feigned a mere calm obeisance to better strike at a time of his own choosing. Two male servants in the household who protested the substitution of some paintings in the attic for the more valuable ones in the house, were peremptorily dismissed, as witnessed by the guards.

There was a legal wrinkle, however, because perhaps of a lapse committed by the drafters of Lauro's English will. That document, which carries a date posterior to the Italian will (thus technically invalidating the one executed in Rome), made no mention of the Polish Institute—a fact that gave the lawyers for the latter some reason to lose sleep, and sealed a perennial antipathy toward the American university's binational legal "team." In Italy, the Poles had legal title, but that could be contested if the American will were enforced, thus leaving them at the mercy of the American set, which was, by that same token, suspect of fraud. Among members of the legal profession, one thing is to be a crook; another, no doubt worse, is to be a careless rogue.

The whole unsavory mess was kept under wraps for a year or two, until one day, Alberto, in whom the inexorable illness and the quest for revenge burned with equal haste, decided to talk. He struck at the weakest link in the entire chain of misdeeds, and confronted Lorenzo, whom he had known also intimately well, as they were all in the same circle of "friends." Alberto did not mince his words: he let Lorenzo know, in unequivocal terms, that he knew all about the theft, and was ready to speak to the authorities too, unless he was given a handsome *stipendio*, to ease the end of his days. There were shouts, threats, and tears, and in the end, a tenuous settlement was reached. Lorenzo was frightened, lost all sleep, and confided in Daz that he was being blackmailed. It was a fatal misstep. Daz took the confidence in stride, but his devious mind soon started to work.

Two murders then follow such sequence of events: one successful, the second one foiled. They both involve, respectively, what in the detective trade is called a setup, or "frame." First, Lorenzo succumbs to a hard blow to the head, and to a powerful stranglehold. His corpse is discovered, one early afternoon, floating in the fountain of a nearby park known as a gay cruising ground, his throat slit, nibbled by gold fish and lept over by frogs. The police make inquiries, follow some leads, and soon all fingers point to a *crime passionel*, a lovers' dispute, everybody says, or a casual encounter with a brute. "This is not uncommon in Le Cascine, Florence's notorious park. That is how the crime appears in the press. The journalists described the activities in the park—a favorite place for what Italians call *battuage*, and the French *drague*—in lurid detail:

Qui si possono incontrare i cosiddetti «passeggiatori». Uomini che non frequentano normalmente le prostitute, ma che si divertono a guardare gli altri e, quando capita, a partecipare attivamente agli incontri proibiti. (Here one can meet so-called leisurely walkers, men who do not normally frequent prostitutes, but amuse themselves in watching other men, and when the moment is propitious, actively participate in forbidden encounters.)

The press reported a failed "romantic liaison" which ended tragically, one of many that occur in big cities, although usually it is an older man that ends up dead: he meets a younger man one night, brings him home for what he believes is a night of sex and fun, and instead is bashed on the head, stabbed to death, and robbed as well.

But someone appears who remains unconvinced. It is the new director of the villa, in charge of the estate, and in seeming possession, through his own research, of most relevant facts about the past art heist. He is the quiet yet relentless Professor Lynch, who strikes up a friendship with the chief detective, Nino Lanza, of the Polizia dello Stato. In a series of meetings in the estate, followed by meals in little restaurants in the old Roman ghetto, in rides to the city and back in a zippy old Alfa, these two dogged characters rearrange the facts and produce a new suspect from their notes—none other than Daz.

They realize that the corpse found with a slit throat had actually been strangled before the stabbing and in some other site and then brought quite cold to the park, hence the meager loss of blood for a wound of that nature. In the clasped hand of the deceased, they found a button that corresponded to a loden coat similar to one usually worn by Daz and which probably had been torn in the struggle that preceded death. But the master puppeteer has covered all traces, made the loden disappear, and there was no clear way to expose him, except by a clever tease designed to offer him a new murder bait.

They set up a trap, which entails grave danger. Professor Lynch is to let Daz know that *he* has discovered what had taken place between Lorenzo and Alberto, and suggest that it is only the tip of an iceberg. Daz should be properly upset. The director will thus place himself in the line of fire, while the inspector will secretly follow every move by Daz, every scheme he might hatch to get rid of the professor.

After some hesitation—hence narrative suspense—Daz conceives a plan, calls on two accomplices, a sinister lawyer—Alfonso Scaletta—and a venal architect—Rudolph Zimmerbang—who, together with Daz, had for several years bilked the estate. The unholy trinity plans to entice the director toward what will seem an unfortunate accident, a fatal *disgrazia*. The lawyer will summon the director to inspect the ceilings of the old lemonary in the vegetable garden. The architect will accompany Lynch to the site and point to a broken beam above the crown-shaped iron chandelier that is hung from it. As the two stand below observing the crack, the architect's cell phone will ring, and he will then excuse himself to chat in a corner of the vast shed. At that precise moment, the beam will seem to move, to crack, and the entire bulk of crown and lamp, triggered by a hidden Daz, will come crashing down on the director's head. (Daz had always remarked that the professor took on princely airs; hence, by this method of death, he would indeed be crowned.)

Lanza instructs the professor to follow the script to his expected doom while he shadows Daz in all preparations, making sure that the lamp, after Daz's engineering, is secured by a double length of chain, so that when it falls, it does not drop too far. He finally places several undercover agents, parading as workers, near the doubly booby-trapped site. When, literally, the dust has settled, and the professor is saved, Gabor, caught *in flagrante delicto*, is promptly put away, soon to be followed by his two accomplices, and by major scandals in Rome, Chicago, and Warsaw.

The entire sketch, whose sequence must be rearranged, of course, to produce the desired effect of mystery, is in fact based on a little fable by Borges, taken from Dr. Samuel Johnson, which boils down to this: Two gentlemen meet. One mocks and insults the other, in the guise of a concerned alert. 'Sir, your wife, under pretense of keeping a bawdy house, is a receiver of stolen goods.'"

Candido enjoyed the plot but wasn't sure if Harold invented it before or after his death. Was it Harold's dream, or his? And what are dreams: products of a mind that lost its guard, or messages from another realm, as ancient Greeks thought? Who knows? Be that as it may, Candido decided to take it as a warning. The two deaths foretold in the draft never took place, but a third one did.

In any case, Candido now had something more and more ominous to worry about in the villa—namely, the trail of past art theft. Had it actually taken place? And whodunnit? He started to check records, reconstruct events, and question the older members of the staff, especially the gardeners. The resolution of those mysteries—though always inconclusive—would not come until his wife and he had left the villa and their jobs, tired of being undermined by what it had seemed to them at the time a misguided but honest policy by their bosses. And yet, not a fictional but a real, public, and rather spectacular death opened their eyes to something else. It took place while they were exiting Europe on their sailboat through the Straits of Gibraltar and had other adventures—both happy and sad—in South and North America, and in the Orient too.

In Which a Visit to the Villa Gives Rise to a Conversation About Dealership in Art

There were four visitors that morning, friends of a friend of the vice president for institutional affairs of the university. They were sportily dressed, not too garrulous, and somewhat intimidated by the halls. As usual, Maria gave the tour of the villa and its collection. Candido teased her, calling this duty of hers, which she actually enjoyed, "the Jackie-Kennedy-at-the-White-House routine." He trailed behind her and her tourists to have a conversation with an old classmate from his college days in Massachusetts, who was also visiting the villa.

"Did you know much about art and dealing before you took the Florence job?"

"Well, I had only some scholarly clues, due to my interest in art criticism. But that was an innocent view. In those days, art meant to me only aesthetic appreciation, a form of elevating oneself as part of spiritual cultivation—what the Germans called *Bildung*. I am sure you remember."

"At Brandeis University, music appreciation was one of my favorite courses, and the teacher was none other than Aaron Copland. On the visual arts, we had another great teacher: Leo Bronstein."

"It was only in the 1980s, during the great boom in the art market, that I knew some people who actually made art deals. A suave, ruthless, piratical crowd. I was a stranger to this fauna, until in New York, Athens, and Paris, I met a few."

"Did they talk to modest professors like you?"

"Wouldn't give them the hour of day. But I have a friend, also from our college time, whom I keep seeing since then, who became one of them, buying and selling Impressionists for ship owners in those halcyon days. She would invite me during summers to sail with them in the Aegean. She entertained them on her boat. I was an old friend who handled the sheets, took us out of port, helped with the drinks, and shuttled between five languages with ease. That helped."

"You had some credentials then."

"Just a few. I always taught a course on art and society, which put forth an outsider's—a barbarian's—point of view. This villa introduced me to a different sort of nitty-gritty, to the seamier side of art."

"I am intrigued by your apprenticeship."

"It was involuntary, forced by circumstance. I was thrown into a pool with sharks."

"But you survived."

"One of my predecessors at the villa did not. She was married to an art dealer who smuggled a Rubens to America, from a princely collection, made a false move, and was caught. Guilt by association, fatal in that world."

"You had to do some homework then."

"It was essential, a survival tool. At first, I drew on old memories from college, when a group of us, remember?—in the blush of our youth—listened, fascinated, to Leo Bronstein tell us about *his* youth in France. He was a charming gadfly, our Gombrich, our guru. Such was Brandeis in 1962."

"Old stuff. What happened to that world?"

"Most of our teachers are dead: Bronstein himself, but also Copland, Marcuse, Maslow, Kitto, Popper, Eleanor Roosevelt, Abba Eban, C. Wright Mills."

"And the rest of us? What became of our jolly band of class-mates, many of them foreigners, thanks to scholarships funded by Larry Wien?"

"There's a billionaire in Kuala Lumpur, a king of cement in Japan, a putschist who rots in jail in Grenada, a gentle Vietnamese who developed GPS; the rest are architects, nuclear physicists, pianists, professors and deans, moviemakers, and many whose traces I have lost. But those were days of yearning, days of learning!"

"*Dies illa*, those were the days. I have fond memories."

"Me too, but today I brood instead and remember the full Gregorian chant: the day of wrath, the day that will dissolve the world in ashes."

"Better stick to the past."

"We sat around Leo, late at night, drank coffee, and listened to the man tell us about a magic world across the seas. Famous names came alive in his words: great artists, their loves, their agents, their quirks, and their escapades.

"Leo told us that a great many people got into the art business after the war. Art was a wondrous thing, but art dealing was not always clean, not in a period when thousands of works of art were drifting around the continent, their owners dead, some in the Shoa, or lost or forgotten. A great deal of money could be made if someone knew what he or she was doing and didn't mind cutting a few corners. Even the great living artists did the same. Picasso paid for his meals by drawing on napkins, and flamboyant Dali was known among his friends by the clever rearrangement of the letters in his name: *Avida Dollars* they called him. Among old art dealers, some were expert and honest—*rara avis*, Leo would say. Most were expert corner-cutters, cheap cheats. Florence was full of them, some parading behind fancy names.

"Look at this villa: it's a house museum by half; the other half is Ali Baba's cave. With his pretensions, and his wife's money, the man who assembled the collection for this palace purchased some good pieces, but others were a joke. He called them "editions" or "authentic reproductions." He clearly bought and sold some dubious art, and sometimes fobbed newly made fakes onto suckers for high prices."

"Was this unique?"

"No. Standard practice. Run of the mill. It ran like this. Sculptors of ancient busts and painters of old masters worked for such dealers in various corners of Italy, many with excellent skills. Then there were the agents who assiduously plundered the galleries and collections of the country to stock new, wealthy, and hungry American museums."

"Do you think the situation has changed?"

"With ever-fewer pieces to find—these are no longer the giddy days of Berenson and Duveen—more legal obstacles to plunder, and ever-higher prices to ask, the situation is a bit tighter today."

"How does it work then?"

"A typical player would be someone born, like us, in the 1940s, educated in the US or the UK, who worked as a dealer until employed by a rich collector, became curator of the collection, then chief buyer in Europe based in Rome, Geneva, Paris, or London. An acquisition by this buyer might very well be a perfect head by Bernini, a little-known Franz Hals, or a jovial Rubens. I could even picture how it goes." Candido then imitated them, probably from snippets once heard on my friend's yacht:

"Superb, undoubtedly genuine. Excellent condition. I can let you have my written assessment, if you want."

"Thank you. I'd like to see it. Where did it come from?"

"That's a bit sensitive."

"Why is that?"

"Confidential. The owners are most insistent. Family matter, I suppose."

"The unknown seller is one of the old tricks in the book for covering up smuggled goods."

"Exactly. The authorities have usually a hard time trying to pin the smiling, Armani clad crook down. The buyer sees and hears no evil. He bought it fairly, and the museum paid for it when it arrived in America. As far as smuggling goes, well, the circuitous route, the change of hands, makes it hard to trace.

"It is the same with arms. Art and weapons have an elective affinity, don't you think?"

"They are very expensive toys, much sought after."

"There's plenty of dirty cash around, searching to be laundered."

"But sometimes there is a lead, an indiscretion is heard, or a whistle blown. Rivalries and vendettas abound in the art world."

"And a dogged investigator strikes gold, securing the long sought-for promotion at last."

"It is not an easy task, and, as in most police investigations, dumb luck plays its part. Sometimes the most the authorities can do is fine the owner for smuggling, but not if the 'discreet family' (pressed for cash) sold in plausible good faith, ignoring the final destination. On the other hand, if the first purchaser (a dealer) offers it in turn—at an extraordinarily inflated price—to a foreign buyer, and makes arrangements to deliver—without applying, of course, for an export permit—and is paid, he or she can be said verily to have broken the law, and usually more than one. At that precise and dangerous point, the folks at the *Belle Arte*, the national police, the tax officers, and Interpol, all sink their fangs into the dealer's flesh."

"What happens then?"

"The American museum is appropriately surprised."

"Bullshit, wouldn't you say?"

"Yes, but it solemnly promises to send it back, and makes claims for restitution of the large sum wired to one or several accounts, in Zurich, in Monaco, or in Liechtenstein. *Noblesse oblige*, you understand, and not a word about the eagerness, the haste in declaring the object a genuine masterpiece, the ballooned price, the potential loss. It has lawyers, good accountants, insurance, and a PR department for all that. If, by chance, another expert studies the object, and expresses serious doubts about its authenticity: What if it were "from the school of" rather than from the very master's brush, an exact version made long ago, same century perhaps, out of sheer devotion, but no doubt after the master's death, or a freshly concocted fake? Then in America, it can be kept, and there has been no other crime than, if it could ever be proven, conspiracy to defraud. The so-called masterpiece lands in a climate-controlled vault in California, waiting patiently for the joyful day of resurrection."

"Now yes, let me complete the reference: *Dies irae, dies illa, solvet saeclum in favilla.*"

Candido's friend continued in translation (he knew the Mass):

"The day of wrath, that day
will dissolve the world in ashes,

How great will be the quaking,
when the Judge is about to come,
strictly investigating all things.'

With some effort, Candido put it back in the liturgical Latin. It came from Mozart' Requiem, he confessed:

Quantus tremor est futurus,
Quando Judex est venturus,
Cuncta stricter discursurus!'

"I get it: a future expert opinion, a different approach, new techniques, public acclaim, and a fortune restored, many years hence."
"Precisely."
"The future of art is in art futures then."
"In this business, my boy, there's money in futures, and a good chunk of the future is the past. It is a dizzying world in which fraudulent originals are hard to distinguish from false fakes. Nothing is what it seems."
At the end of the tour, the visitors were offered a glass of *prosecco* and a few *tramezzini*. Candido's friend parted in jovial terms. The other visitors seemed relieved, politely thankful, and a bit pressed to leave (they were ordered a cab). They wanted badly to go back shopping on the via Tornabuoni.

EPISODE 15

The Last Supper

POTUS and FLOTUS come to town

For Candido, it all seemed like a fairy tale, taking place in a villa where so many tales of fairies were held. But the event became more real by the day, during the long summer months when it was prepared. Every detail was discussed and then planned for execution. Advance parties came and went. The estate was inspected for security, the buildings checked with a fine comb. Government sherpas, various bodies of police, intelligence agents, and the Secret Service all came—even the pilot of Air Force One, with whom Candido had a candid talk about survival techniques on land and at sea.

After everything and everybody were ready, the midsummer night's dream took place in the late fall. When it happened, the century and the millennium were coming to a close. Y2K loomed large, and not without foreboding.

What made it possible was to a considerable extent a wife's tale. It seemed that the wife of a dean at Global U. was friends with the wife of the American president, and this auspicious detail made it possible for the villa—now a US "facility" of prestige—to be offered as the site for a grand celebratory dinner.

To celebrate what? Nothing less than the triumph of the West. Europe became one; the US had no challengers; Russia was pushed around and to the sides, and China was turned into the universal factory of cheap goods. Like Winston Churchill (twice a guest at the villa in the 1920s), the invited guests knew that "In War, Resolution;

121

In Defeat, Defiance; In Victory, Magnanimity; and in Peace, Good Will." After NATO'S help in dismembering Yugoslavia, it was time to show grace and generosity in a unipolar world where capitalism and democracy reigned supreme and signaled the glorious end of history—not Hegel's end of history but John Philip Sousa's Stars and Stripes Forever.

Seven heads of state had been invited to attend a meeting in Florence to discuss how the world could transit from one century to another in peace, prosperity, and a healthier distribution of life chances. With the strong endorsement of the White House, they could not but accept. In general, it all made sense but it did not go beyond good wishes and some platitudes prepared for the occasion by a few scholars eager for recognition and with a predisposition to comply.

The theme of the symposium was "progressive government for the twenty-first century." Only progressives would attend. They headed governments committed, like Pangloss, to making the best of all possible worlds. They vowed to combine concern for the public weal with continued support of private wealth. They called it the third way, as promoted by a sociologist guru whose entire career was devoted to translating Germanic and French speculation into Anglo-Saxon common sense. From experience, Candido remained skeptical. He knew that the century which was about to end was a cemetery of third positions in a Manichean universe. To him, playing *tertius gaudens* was the errand of fools. At best, it was a means of shedding a kind light on a voyage of power that had required compromise and conversion but never a real synthesis. As with the common rules of driving on the Continent, you enter the car from the left, and you drive on the right. *Sic transit Gloria mundi.*

When they arrived, the city was in lockdown mode. Security personnel were everywhere; hotels were commandeered, for the retinues were big: the British PM was accompanied by, besides his wife, more than a dozen ministers; the German chancellor had only five; the French premier twelve; the Portuguese leader just a few. The Italian *presidente del Consiglio* moved around as if here were at home, which he was (although Candido suspected he was not treated seriously). He was a veteran Communist functionary that had evolved with the times, and morphed into a social-democratic operator and quiet profiteer. The president of Brazil, whom Candido knew well from his professional life before the man left academia for a successful rise to the very heights of politics, was accompanied by no less than fifty people, half of them from the well-reputed Itamaraty (the Ministry of Foreign Affairs). It was a bit of tropical exuberance, but it paled by comparison with the American delegation. POTUS and FLOTUS came with two planes, carrying five hundred minions and friends in the last junket of the presidency. That alone spoke volumes about the imperial strength of the last remaining superpower.

Florence became a festive and protected pod of chitchat and mutual adulation. For three days, it was a city like Siena, meant for pedestrians. But these were not common tourists. For three days, the city gave the impression that it was once again at the center of world history, like in Medicean times. It had all the brilliance and fugacity of a capital soap bubble.

Candido helped with the arrangements, and surrendered his handsome office for three hours to the president of the United States—black boxes, red phone, and all. Candido's secretary had befriended a young woman from Washington D.C. during the summer preparations. Much to the secretary's and Candido's surprise, that evening, the lady came dressed like a black ninja and carried a long rifle, with which she took position on the roof with the other sharpshooters. Then, at precisely 1800 hours, the delegations arrived in a well-choreographed ballet, along the majestic gran viale (great avenue) festooned by old cypress trees, and were received at the door by the authorities of Global U. The other guests came behind the leaders' caravans, in processional buses reserved for the occasion.

Everyone was in a cheery mood, except one. FLOTUS had been humiliated by a sex scandal that led to the impeachment of her mate and power partner. The media had a feeding frenzy, and the dignity of the Oval Office was stained in more ways than one. The Europeans, as opposed to the puritanical Americans, were more amused than scandalized. They had long been tolerant of such peccadillos of the flesh. The French had learned to turn deviant habits into normal routines not worthy of notice, and the Italians trailed not far behind. Once, the president of France was driving his car in the evening in the Bois de Boulogne when the vehicle broke down. Instead of picking up a lady of the night, he had to hitch a ride from a milk truck, which dutifully took him to the Élysée Palace, without any scandal at all. The newspapers did not make much of the episode, which remained a discreet story shared occasionally by word of mouth.

Not so in America. FLOTUS suffered in silence, kept a straight, nay a stone, face, and set her sights on something more important. One day she would become POTUS herself. Revenge is a dish best served cold, and cold she was that evening, although the food was warm, preparing a set of well-calculated moves step-by-step until she reached the prized objective. *A long march begins with the first step, and her presence at the villa was perhaps such move*, Candido thought. Candido could not explain why he observed what he observed, but he knew that the will to power can be stronger than sex. He recalled Henry Kissinger's claim that "power is the ultimate aphrodisiac."

The food was good—not great, but good enough. The conventional caterer of the grandees of Florence had been replaced by a lesser company from Prato. But they performed well—a feat in itself, since it involved feeding near three hundred diners under a tent, over the terraces outside the villa, and extending to the grounds. The tent was heated and well served, with a table of honor surrounded by the rest, each one holding ten guests. It reminded Candido of the magnificent tents that the New York Yacht Club pitched on the grounds of Harbour Court, overlooking the sea and the splendid yachts bobbing at their moorings, in Newport, Rhode Island. Under them, the club could serve two hundred lobsters with impeccable taste.

Candido was largely ignored as he moved from group to group and drink to drink during the cocktail hour that preceded *la grande bouffe*. He knew quite a few people, and recognized many more, luminaries attracted to Florence for the glittery occasion, like butterflies to the light. He saw l'avoccato Agnelli supported by a cane, but keeping an imposing demeanor even in old age, the blind tenor

Andrea Boccelli who sang an aria that night, and the comedian Benigni sauntering from group to group. *Every court must have its clown*, Candido thought.

Candido had a wicked little plan that nobody suspected. A few years before, while in America, he had bought a racing sailboat from a distinguished lawyer in Little Rock, Arkansas. The lawyer and his wife were friends and strong supporters of the presidential couple. When Candido managed to approach POTUS, he introduced himself with all due respect and then said: "Mr. President, let me convey the best wishes from our common friend Matt."

The expression on the president's face changed, and he responded, "Let's go to a corner and chat." And for five minutes, they exchanged jokes and anecdotes—about boats, and legal firms, and failed investments, and yes, girls—as if they had long been friends. As their common friend Matt once told Candido: "You can get the boy out of Little Rock, but you cannot get Little Rock out of the boy."

The other occasion when Candido enjoyed himself that evening was his reunion in, of all places, Florence, with his former colleague and now head of state in Brazil. There were also some less attractive recognitions, as when Candido saw in his own villa an American middle-aged official that he had seen in the audience every time he lectured in Latin America, and most particularly Caracas, where he had been invited by then foreign minister Simon Alberto Consalvi to give a talk on inter-American relations. On that occasion, Candido explained why, of all the countries in Central America, the only stable democratic republic was the one that had escaped from the US anti-communist zeal in the fifties. In fact, Costa Rica had a successful middle-class revolution in 1947 that by some quirk of fate had not been overthrown by the CIA. As a result, it had established Western institutions, abolished the army, and lived happily ever since. Such subversive argument had not gone well with the American in the audience who was monitoring him, and who no doubt reported to the three-lettered institution back home.

The evening went along without incident, after two speeches by POTUS and the PM of the UK. Both were charming, eloquent, and did not say much that was memorable in the dark century that was about to dawn.

The next day was cleanup day at the villa, and Candido was ready for his final act.

EPISODE 16

In Which the Director Quits His Job
in a Swift and Spectacular Way

Candido thought his farewell speech was clever but also well behaved—goodbye from a good boy. He delivered it with poise although he was raging inside with anger. It was composed in the heat of the moment, the very night that followed a rather tacky postmortem celebration of a successful summit with seven heads of state that included POTUS and FLOTUS, and which Candido had helped plan to show what the villa could become. The event was planned rather surreptitiously with the help of a dean that had close connections to the White House. The meeting and dinner were attended by the top echelon of Global U—since it was an affair they could not refuse, despite the fact that it was insubordination on Candido's part.

Backslapping, little speeches of self-congratulation, and thanks profusely proffered to every possible sycophant and to the staff—and the studied offense to the director, who was not mentioned at all. It was a distasteful display of spurious intimacy and resentment. In the background: Irish music, drunken dancing around the baron's desk, and pizza with champagne. In a corner, a confirmed nonsmoker was lighting another philistine's cigar, who received the light with almost postcoital satisfaction, judging from the smug faces. In the foreground: hyperbole, or rather, the weird sincerity of intellectual sociopaths, convinced that when they speak, truth is an option but convenience an imperative.

Candido had had enough. He took Maria's hand, and they climbed the stairs to their apartment. They played a disc by Frank Sinatra, and danced to it.

> I've loved, I've laughed and cried.
> I've had my fill; my share of losing.
> And now, as tears subside,
> I find it all so amusing.

Then Candido sat at Cardinal Capponi's desk, the best piece of furniture in the apartment, and drafted his farewell speech, fortified by a good single-malt, sixteen years old. It turned out postmodern, and tongue-in-cheek. He printed it, folded it, put it in the pocket of his jacket, and delivered it the following morning, at the official inauguration of one of the buildings in the estate, before students, professors, directors of other programs, the entire staff, and the press.

A crowd had gathered to attend the inauguration of villa number four on the day that followed the gathering of the grandees. The remaining chiefs of Global U, the staff, the faculty, the students, the press, and the just curious lingered in the wake of the summit, eager to trade gossip, all feeling important witnesses to a historic event. The ceremony was brief. One vice president said a few words and then introduced Candido, who was supposed to speak about the strides of the university in Florence. He took some sheets that he had tucked in his coat pocket with pointers for the speech.

"One score and three months ago [echoes of the Gettysburg address], when I was asked to assume the directorship of Global University in Florence, the estate was not on my map. The challenge was so interesting, however, that I readily postponed other plans and came.

"When I came, the estate and its villas were in a state of suspended animation: the main palace had the charm of an untouched and magic place. The gardens exuded the scents of ninety years. Two of the other four villas were rented commercially. There was a handful of students, a small faculty, and two classrooms in one of them. Charming and intimate as all this was, signs of stasis and decay showed here and there. The program and the site required strong and judicious restoration and development. Twenty-three months later, we have done this:

- The first three phases of eleven in the restoration of the main historic villa are complete. (We boxed the art and hid the mess.)
- Villa number two is a charming residence hall. (Don't look too close.)
- Villa number three is undergoing a massive restoration and restructuring so that it may house, next year, more than one hundred students. (Not a hint of my shudders at the looming prospect of Club Ed.)
- The gardens are being restored as well, through a meticulous and clear program with the best experts in the world. (They will be used as a playground for young adults, so the wonderful restoration will end in queer Californication.)
- The staff has grown through the addition of top people, and we now have a full and efficient organization (with Rube Goldberg presiding).
- Villa number four is our academic center. It is the jewel that we are officially inaugurating today. It serves 208 students, 36 faculty members, and houses two programs every semester and several others in the summer. (too many, too fast, and at great spiritual price]. Through the efforts of my wife (she too had been unthanked and much maligned), we have a curriculum that we can feel proud of.
- As for the future, we can see the arrival of graduate programs, postgraduate research, and exchange activities, and a program of conferences that will have a vision, a mission, and integrity. On the horizon too, I see the realization of the fundraising potential of this site. (Pipe dreams and pious hopes. But what the hell, this is my swansong.)
- Last but not least, Florence considers our branch as one of its own institutions. The university is respected and bet-

ter understood in the community (for that, I deserve the Purple Heart).

In short, I can say, quoting Winston Churchill, that we have arrived at the end of the beginning.

And now, the end is near;
And so I face the final curtain.
My friend, I'll say it clear,
I'll state my case, of which I'm certain.

"And now that the end is near, my friends, I must face my final curtain." (Sinatra bis.) Candido paused for a sort of shuddering silence. An audience captured in this way belongs to the speaker. Then he delivered the snapper. "I have decided to step down as executive director, beginning exactly on January 1, 2000." He hurled the word-bomb. The house came down with a crash. Members of the staff sobbed; others sighed or gaped. The Italian journalists asked for a translation. Cameras flashed. "I will resume old tasks on my agenda, which I postponed when I came here. I am confident that the organization in place will easily withstand a change in leadership. Allow me a nautical metaphor. I would like to think of my role in Florence as that of an icebreaker. The path is open. Other ships may follow.

Regrets, I've had a few;
But then again, too few to mention.
I did what I had to do
And saw it through without exemption.

I planned each charted course;
Each careful step along the byway,
But more, much more than this,
I did it my way.

Yes, there were times, I'm sure you knew
When I bit off more than I could chew.
But through it all, when there was doubt,
I ate it up and spit it out.
I faced it all and I stood tall;
And did it my way.

"As I am about to leave for Buenos Aires and Beijing, the opening lyrics of a tango come to mind: "*Hoy vas a entrar en mi pasado.*"
"Today you shall enter my past." But now, in joy, let us think of the
future, cut the ribbon, and usher ourselves into the coming century,
nay millennium.

I've lived a life that's full.
I've traveled each and ev'ry highway;
But more, much more than this,
I did it my way.

To think I did all that;
And may I say—not in a shy way,
Oh no not me,
I did it my way.

"Goodbye and God bless."

From an inside coat pocket, Candido then extracted another
envelope, this one containing his official resignation. He ceremoni-
ously delivered it to the vice president in attendance, who could not
dissimulate his stupor. "But…" Then he came down from the stairs
whence he spoke, and left, followed by a swarm of journalists and
well-wishers buzzing around him like bees.

For what is a man, what has he got?
If not himself, then he has naught.
To say the things he truly feels;
And not the words of one who kneels.

The record shows I took the blows—
And did it my way.

Exit the outsider. The prisoners of the palace are free.

Candido's parting words were lost in translation. An Italian journalist for *La Nazione* produced a misspoken farewell. She assumed "good riddance" was akin to "good luck" or "God bless," and quoted him as saying "thank you, goodbye, and good riddance." Hegel would have thought it was no doubt the work of the cunning of reason.

> Today you're gonna enter in my past,
> in the past of my life.
> Three things bears my wounded soul:
> Love, Regret, Pain.
> Today you're gonna enter my past,
> today we'll follow new paths.
> How great has been our love
> and, yet, alas,
> look what's left!
> (Enrique Cadicamo, *Los Mareados,* 1942)

In Which a Death Is Linked to the Villa, and the Death Itself Covers a Perfect Crime

Tosca II

The downfall

The new millennium dawned, and a year passed after Candido and Maria had tendered their resignations from the Florentine assignments. Their resignations in no way meant an abandonment of Florence, where they had so many friends. In one of their subsequent visits, Candido managed to contact the ghost of Harold again—in the same dark room full of hissing steam. He told him about the fatal accident—*la disgrazia*—that shook the university in Chicago and rumor blamed on foul play.

"Did the post-mortem inquiry leave a dribble of doubt?" he asked.

"There are no records of an autopsy, and cremation took care of the remains."

"You and I have been avid readers of detective stories. The first forty-eight hours of a suspect death are crucial. Revealing details are still fresh. If they are spoiled or covered up, the trail is lost."

"I know. After that, witnesses are already jumbling facts, and alibis have been set up. Above all, stories which might conflict are adjusted."

"Especially in an institution with a well-established PR department."

"So there is no way to know if she died before or after the fall."

"All I remember is the statement of someone in her entourage: 'she was pushed to do it.' Other statements, in anonymous phone calls to her office, were much more crass: 'ding-dong, the witch is gone.'"

"The official version is that she was deeply depressed, and jumped to her death from a tenth-floor balcony."

"I would rather say distressed. She was not the suicidal type."

"Distressed by what?"

"She was set up. She was made the fall guy in a scandal involving stolen goods."

"If she was killed, then it was a murder out of place," the ghost said.

Candido liked the phrase.

"Out of place?"

"For reasons that were two thousand miles from where it took place."

"Maybe, but I always think of an Italian journey as a round trip."

"If she was killed, the killers are no longer in America, but back here."

"You mean in Florence?"

"No, more likely in the rolling hills of Caltanissetta."

"You think the Mafia was involved?"

"The Mafia is blamed for everything in Italy."

At that point, Candido remembered the lines from Dr. Johnson, from Borges, and from Harold himself, and quoted them again: "Sir, your wife under pretense of keeping a bawdy house, is a receiver of stolen goods." That was the clue.

He thought he heard the ghost giggle.

"She made two mistakes that led to her very literal downfall. She picked the wrong bawdy house and chose the wrong kind of stolen goods."

"The house was too big, too known, too visible in its distinction to be treated like that. You can't bring New Jersey to Florence like a juggernaut."

"Tell me more."

"I told you she was a preponderant, pushing person, large in arrangement, imperious in overture, and prone to fits of rage, which she vented on submissive ladies in waiting, her assistants. Every time they descended on the villa, it was a nightmare. They ordered everybody around invoking their mistress, munched fast food, and slept in the historic bedrooms of the palace."

"Don't say: my beloved Blue Room, the one I always reserved for Princess Margaret and her Grundig radio?"

"Yes, and the Yellow Room as well."

"The one where Charles and Diana spent part of their honeymoon!"

"By coincidence, perhaps those two ladies in waiting were both morbidly obese. One of them insisted she had to sleep in the Blue Room. It had to be prepared for her, lest one incurred her wrath and the hatred of her boss, who was, for all practical purposes, the first lady of Global U. That night, in an emergency, she could not find a bathroom in the dark, and dumped the contents of her guts on the marble floor."

"Oh dear!"

"There is more. The next morning, before an astonished cleaning lady, she blamed the mishap on Candido's and Maria's dog, the faithful Bonaparte. They let it pass, but thought that their beloved springer spaniel would have had to morph into a Great Dane to accomplish such discharge."

"And the mistress?"

"She fancied herself a charismatic woman like Evita, although she looked more like Mme. Milosevic, and just as coy. This annual visit had upon the villa staff the same effect as a visit by a dominatrix. They were tortured, humiliated, and abused. She had a special place: the building next to the master house which she had disposed as her own boudoir at the estate's expense. Every spring, she flew from America to this eagle's nest whence she ruled in the name of her boss—a fatuous president of Global U that she had long made comfortable in many ways and whom she led by the nose. It was bad enough, but it was not this abuse that led her to a sorry fate. She got involved in a dubious import-export trade, with shady characters on each end."

"Please continue."

"I was the director, but she didn't give a hoot. I found out that during the restoration of one of the villas in the estate, she ordered the removal of all the antique furniture and its replacement by 'new stuff' imported from America. I was out of the loop."

"Tacky, but to be expected."

"She bypassed all normal channels. It was irregular and in terrible taste, but not a crime, just one more of her many mistakes—until I discovered that the antique furniture had vanished under the guise of repair or restoration, and sold somewhere with no records of traceable proceeds."

"Did you denounce it?"

"I officially asked for an inquiry and a report, and got nowhere—no response, niente, nada, τίποτα, nothing. And then it got worse."

"How so?"

"One afternoon in the early months of my tenure, I received the visit of a circumspect old gentleman. He looked like Mr. Carson in Downton Abbey. He wanted to introduce himself and bring his good wishes. He had been chief of the villa staff for quite some time. Is that true?"

"Yes, of course. He was my faithful Sandro! By the time he left without even saying goodbye, I had declined in body and mind, was very tired, and my secretary took over the daily management of the property. I was confined to a wheelchair, and my secretary took it upon himself to redecorate some rooms and move some of the art around. I had no strength to intervene, so I let him do it."

"Did you know that some pieces went to the attic, and some paintings in the attic replaced them?"

"Nobody told me, and I was half asleep most of the time to notice."

"They were brought downstairs by two of the *camarieri*, the orderlies under the gentleman's command—Sandro you said was his name?—but he had no say in it. A few other works of art were packaged with care and delivered by the same *camarieri* to an antiquarian's shop in the Lungarno, allegedly for cleaning or repair. He felt it was odd, especially as the art did not come back, and as what was in the attic vanished as well."

"Oh god… I suspected something like that would happen one day, so I wrote the script that you found and which you say has been lost. By the time it actually happened, I was too *imbecillito* to realize it. And that involved blackmail and murder too."

"It looks that way: uncannily prescient."

"I am amazed. What strange force leads us sometimes to foretell the future?"

"When I was little a nun, sister Manuela, said to me one day, 'God never leads his children otherwise than they would choose to be led, if they could see the end from the beginning, and discern the purpose which they are fulfilling as coworkers with him.'"

"I know that now quite well. But please continue."

"Shortly thereafter, under one pretext or another, the *camarieri* were fired without asking Sandro's consent, and later yet, he, the old gentleman, was let go as well. He was most distressed, especially when he could not even say goodbye to you, whom he loved and respected, he said. He told me that he wanted to get such sadness out of his chest before a new director whom he hoped would make the villa whole again."

"Poor Sandro. I hope he understands and has forgiven me. But what happened with the vanished art?"

"It's hard to know, but easy to surmise."

"And what did you suspect"

"You see, normally, authorities are in the hunt for stolen art, and for copies that pass for the original pieces, but nobody is very interested in certified, acknowledged fakes."

"What do you mean?"

"I mean that if you manage to spirit away an original, leave behind a well-executed copy or a second-rate equivalent, and export the real thing as a certified fake, you manage to commit an almost-perfect crime."

"Not quite perfect. I seem to remember there was an inventory somewhere."

"Ah, that is the master stroke! What if there wasn't, or was too old, or forgotten, but they manage to have a most prestigious house like Sotheby's or Christie's do an exhaustive inventory of what is there *after* the heist? From then on, that inventory becomes the official list of the collection, and of course nobody can touch it."

"A perfectly legal cover-up. The clever bastards…"

"I did find one hole in the cover-up. I once laid my eyes on a fairly exhaustive list of belongings at the villa drawn by punctilious Fascist authorities in 1941, after Italy requisitioned the property as belonging to 'enemy citizens.'"

"Oh yes, that's the one! My father kept a copy in his desk on the third floor."

"At the time, I was not on the trail of art theft, so I did not photocopy the document, and it too disappeared under unexplained circumstances later on. In fact, I was told it never existed. So the cover-up is still airtight. The mystery remains, the crime took place, nothing can be proven, and the official version is unimpeachable, just as in *Murder in the Orient Express*."

"So you played the part of Hercule Poirot. It happened, but it didn't happen."

"Yes, the clever outsider who uses his little grey cells against the brutality of the world. When I resigned, because I couldn't take it anymore, that is what my friend the Marchesa di Santo Spirito thought."

"I remember her. Beautiful, strong, and very intelligent."

"As I told her, the ship had been taken over by the rats, and I jumped. The night before my very public resignation, I met with her in the kitchen of her palazzo (at the time we were like family) and confessed my intention to leave my job and the villa. She did not object, nor was she surprised. In her mind, resigning was the better option in a dangerous situation, the most dignified, and also the safer one. A most intelligent woman, and a master tactician, she said:

"Caro, you were getting too close to the money, and in these matters, as in many others, one should always follow the money."

"So that was the 'procurement of stolen goods': an international trade in false fakes!"

"It took me quite a bit of time to realize that such was the game. My friend Matteo, who is an art dealer in Old Masters in Milano, explained it to me. I could not prove it, and the goods were probably already abroad and sold for a pittance to those 'in the know.'"

"Now they are quietly waiting for a time when they will be recertified (with a hazy provenance) and sold for millions."

"There is of course a sequel to that story. Someone 'in the know,' for some venal reason, must have threatened to expose the scheme and blackmailed an entire institution all the way to the very top of the cumbersome structure. In the face of it, the only solution was to find an appropriate fall guy, or gal, and thus deflect suspicions. He or she would be 'discovered' and charged."

"But such a person could in turn threaten to expose her higher-ups as a logical defense."

"Precisely. That explains the death by defenestration."

"So what remains a mystery is a mere matter of grammar: is suicide a transitive or an intransitive act?"

"It does not really matter. The fall guy or gal is gone, in a final act of institutional immunization. Everything is where it should be: a tragedy, plausible denial, and talk of 'all is well.'"

"If this had been an Italian opera, the villain would give his victim a choice of death: "*o la coppa, o la spada*": either poisoned chalice or the sword. But there was no choice in America: only the balcony, and a presumption of suicide."

"There is even a happy ending of sorts to the sordid story. *De mortuis nihil nisi bonum* (Only speak well of the dead.)

"For some at the university, she was an unsung heroine. She gave her life for alma mater. In the villa, there is a plaque honoring her."

But Candido knew better: the villa was the special place that the same wrathful God who stuck the baron in his bathhouse purgatory had reserved for her as a private inferno. For the public, she was in heaven; for those who knew, she was in hell, no doubt in Dante's eighth circle, but not sure in which pit.

"Your story reminds me of Borges's *Theme of the Traitor and the Hero.*"

"Well, you know, it was Borges who said that fate loves repetitions. The theme does not change. With Arthur Conan Doyle, Agatha Christie, Magdalen Nabb, Donna Leon, Georges Simenon, and other master writers, it lurks behind many a murder plot."

"Sometimes I get the feeling that most history is a huge cover-up."

EPISODE 18

In Which the Estate Is
Finally Repurposed

A model for the estate

The Denouement

Loss of purpose and loss of income are fatal to an institution when they are combined. As the years went by, with nationalism on the rampage at home—in Italy, the perennial renaissance of fascism—and abroad, and the rapid "trending" of crazy attitudes and alarms in the media, the global university found itself in the midst of a changed geopolitical environment: not liberty, universal amity, and the free exchange of diverse ideas, but mutual suspicion and tribal retrenchment everywhere. Foreign-exchange controls tightened, visas were difficult to get, students from every country refrained from discussing sensitive subjects in front of students from other countries and in front of students from their own home. The more daring among them asked to submit written work touching on issues such as human rights under a pseudonym. Professors—always ready to take abuse from anyone—offered that option to all. America reinvented Russian *samizdat*. Some students reported on their teachers to scared administrators. The greater power of technology meant that it became ever easier for young scholars to remain isolated, mixing little with their peers face-to-face. The volatility of economic conditions in countries here and there made planning at the global university difficult, a condition aggravated by the amateurish fashion—to put it delicately—in which budgets were managed. And then came the pandemic that ravaged the world. For La Gabbia, it was financially the kiss of death.

Before the plagues, the satellite campus had turned into a gated community whence students would "study abroad" by making forays into the surrounding city or countryside, very much like tourists on packaged vacations. It was unsustainable, especially after a year of fearing infection. Travel was suspended. In-class learning was verboten. The hour of decision finally arrived. It was time to divest, pure and simple. The hour arrived in the year 2025 after protracted negotiations in Panama, the US, Italy, and Qatar. Five years later, in 2030, a visit to the campus yielded a different bucolic scene.

In the capacious sitting room of Olivetti Hall, a handsome Florentine *villa finta* (once a peasant house) rebuilt in the 1920s in Renaissance style for an art dealer to rent to an American pulp fiction writer, a tight little group of senior gentlemen is poring over a crossword puzzle. Outside, the sunlit terrace overlooks a lawn that stretched into the distance, over a dale of olive trees, strewn with the yellow dots of spring daffodils. But the puzzlers are not interested in the view—they are too busy consulting a tablet app to unravel clues.

"I hate cryptic crosswords," says Dr. Abdulrahman Bin Abdullah Taleb, eighty, a retired minister of finance of one of the emirates, as he tapped away on the device. "I like plain general knowledge. Keeping the mind going; it's one of the best things."

Hasnain Meriche, Dr. Taleb's bodyguard since the days before the minister fell from grace (they were both detained, charged with sedition, raped, and beaten severely before being deported) strides in, fresh from a morning run. Later he will join other friends similarly employed for tennis before a three-course lunch (goose liver pâté, Sauternes-battered halibut with chunky chips, passion fruit and kiwi platter) with the ex-minister in the dining room.

The minister has lived in Strawberry Hill, Surrey, in a high-end care home for older people, for ten months, after his racehorse estate in Normandy (bought from Stavros Niarchos's heirs) became increasingly difficult to run. But he was not happy there, even though that particular care home sported high-tech bedrooms with smart sensors, a library, a beauty and massage salon, and was reminiscent of a smart hotel, like the Quiberon Sofitel. The home was very expensive by mere mortals' standards, but not for him, who could not possibly spend all the money he had scurried away in Lichtenstein and the Seychelles while managing the finances of that particular emirate. Money was not an issue. Boredom was. Boredom triggered depression, and depression was a road to dementia. He saw it all around him, no matter how wealthy or powerful the posh clients were. Instead, Olivetti Hall is a happier place, bathed in sun, in a beautiful city, and near all the splendors of central Italy.

"The notion that if you need care, you move into a solitary fifteen-foot-square room is very dated," said Jack Berriman, chief executive of the Davos Accommodation Counsel, a Swiss organization that helped high-net-worth individuals find residential care.

Olivetti Hall is not just expensive: it is beyond the reach even of the common rich. Rooms start at $20,000 a week, rising to $50,530 for the largest rooms for residents with the most intensive care needs.

Operated by the Brown River Trust, a provider for the Panama-based corporation that has always nominally owned the estate in a tax-dodging scheme going back to the university days, the first ten-bedroom home opened in 2030 following a $50M refurbishment. It is one of four villas in the estate, each different in age, size, prestige, and disposition, but all offering the same twenty-four-hour residential care. Some residents had dementia, others physical disabilities or limited mobility, a total of one hundred at any given time. What the diverse residents have in common is a powerful past, a need for privacy, and an immense amount of ill-begotten wealth.

The units are designed to attract a class of plutocrats who might have difficulty buying into exclusive properties still hampered by the proprieties of law or custom. The new geopolitical situation has witnessed, in addition to the high-tech telecommunications and start-up booms, the rise of hedge funds, the theft of the former USSR state resources, and the ascendance of China's state-capitalist moguls, also and significantly the displacement of former strongmen (and some strong women) due to either palace coups or popular revolts. Some of them had been in power for decades, and amassed enormous fortunes. Here is a gaping hole at the end of the market begging to be filled, specializing on the senior portion of the very high end. Ease of access had of course attracted shady characters, most of them infamous has-beens. But then, private wealth standards are not what they used to be.

International capital flight has been the decisive impetus in the project and convinced Global U that it was the right time to get rid of this expensive "study abroad" site, beset by legal wrangles and diminishing returns. Most of the new residences (a complete makeover of former student dorms) are paid for entirely in cash. A whole chain of people involved in the sales—lawyers, accountants, brokers, escrow agents, and building workers—many of them connected to trustees, operate with blinders on. The holding corporation doesn't know where the money comes from. It is not interested. The only constraint is, befitting the times, not social, religious, or race bias, let alone conflict of interest—just the depth of pocket. "If I think that the client sold drugs or has blood on his hands, that is where I draw the line. But when it's a guy who has undeclared money, as long as the bank accepts the money and he has a lot of it, I do the deal," says one of the brokers, who speaks on condition of anonymity. Purchasers are required to have liquid assets equal to many multiples of a residence's price, which has limited sales in them to a tiny portion of the top one percent, just perfect for the new development plan.

There appears to be no shortage of individuals prepared to pay the extraordinary premium to live at the old property and its surrounding estate. The managers are so confident demand would increase that they have spent millions upfront in renovating the old Renaissance villa atop the Montughi hill, and also the three ancillary villas on the estate. The entire complex is a fancy gulag of independent and "assisted living" flats and houses—self-contained but with on-site staff and extras such as private spas, gyms, and restaurants.

The estate has also been relandscaped on the model of a Florida wildlife reservation with accommodations for meetings and guests. It is a remarkable plan. In the wildlife reservation, animals are free to roam in the woods and in the fields but are kept from going beyond their pens with guarded fences, and were thus protected from the encroachments of the outside world. In the repurposed campus on the edge of Florence, not the wild but the assisted life of an equally rare species is protected and profitably preserved. In both cases, the idea is to maintain a high-security Eden. From his steamy purgatory, I think Harold sees how his beloved house and estate did not go to hell, but rose to the heaven of a Disney World.

The trust targets a unique niche market: retired tyrants, deposed dictators, exiled oligarchs, sheiks shaken by popular revolts, aging autocrats forced to "downsize" from palaces of power to a tranquil vestibule of paradise, with all the amenities they could imagine that were owed them in the afterlife. It was not just for enfeebled strongmen. Some notorious women were targeted as well, like Africa's richest heiress (her fortune came from Dad who was president almost for life in a country with fabulous wealth underground and abject poverty above it) in search of a non-prosecutorial haven.

When the development was first announced, 85 percent of dwellings were sold off-plan. Typically, clients pay several millions for a hundred-year lease for their portion of one of the four villas—depending on size and prestige. Personal bodyguards, a concierge service, cinema, and spa pool are among the facilities on offer, and again, costs are steep. Besides the sale purchase price, residents pay a service charge fixed at the time of purchase and a deferred membership fee. The latter is payable when the residential unit is sold, and is between 10 and 20 percent of up to 30 percent of the sale price. Residents will never have to worry about cost of living going up or any such trivia, and they have certainty of staying. It is a very exclusive club, *ad vitam*. The best quality auxiliary care may be impossible to buy, but the villa estate comes very close. The trust is convinced that the human touch in care, the feeling that one is at the center of the universe, can indeed be purchased on this magic hill, this Florentine Magic Mountain for crooked billionaires.

It was the litany of financial details that finally woke Candido up. He was puzzled by the dream, but in the twilight zone between sleep and lingering in bed awake, he soon realized what had triggered it the day before. He had given a lecture to incoming freshmen on the texts and ideas of the Western world, and had found a shortcut to explain to them the basic structure of European feudalism. The best analogy, he told them, is with the Mafia. The overlord extracted services and rent from the peasants on his land in exchange for protection from himself and other lords like him. In the distant past, behind every dukedom and earldom stood a protection racket.

After the lecture, in conversation with a colleague, Candido extended the analogy to the college universe. In fact, he told his friend a university administrative class—the captains of learning—had turned American higher education into a monopoly on the sale of valuable credentials, and everybody else, from government to the public, for some time believed their tale. Elite universities are accredited racketeers that use intellectual and economic muscle to scare parents into either paying protection money or risking something awful happening to their children. But over the years, the whole scheme has become less and less sustainable, and so less and less credible.

Given such decadence, why not give up the rotten game altogether and use the villa as a much grander, more profitable cash machine? Why not trade the obsolete model of a Club Ed for pampered and indebted undergraduates for a much more profitable Club Med for the older ultrarich? It would place the estate ahead of the game, when it became obvious that higher education would be accessible almost free, to anybody everywhere, and the values of humanism will rise again (but not on campuses) like phoenix from the ashes of a shabby global interlude.

Aurea mediocritas: the new scheme would be the latest avatar of the five-hundred-year-old property—better than a thermal resort for aching bones: it would be thalassotherapy and thanatotherapy combined.

The dream turned out to be an announcement of things to come. The villa was sold and became a luxury resort for an elderly clientele. As of this writing, a new and tenacious virus is spreading like wildfire in the villa. It is not spared the fate of so many nursing homes.

The end

ABOUT THE AUTHOR

Juan E. Corradi is professor emeritus of sociology at New York University and the author of eight other books. Born and raised in Buenos Aires, in his younger years, he aspired to become the ideal Argentine: an Italian who speaks Spanish, dresses like an Englishman, and lives in Paris. He added Florence to the list. An American, he now lives with his wife, Christina Spellman, in Newport and Manhattan. They love classic boats, fast cars, and English springer spaniels.